"So you need a boyfriend," Rick Serenghetti said without preamble.

She itched to rub the smug smile off his face. "I don't need anything. This would be a completely optional but mutually advantageous arrangement."

And right after this conversation, she was going to have another serious talk with her manager. What had Odele signed her up for?

"You need me."

She burned. He'd made it sound like *You want me.*

"I've been asked to play many roles, but never a stud."

"Don't get too excited."

He grinned. "Don't worry, I won't. I have a thing for the doe-eyed, dark-haired look, but since Camilla Belle isn't available, you'll do."

The flames of temper licked her, not least because he was clued in as to her Hollywood doppelgänger. "So you'll settle?"

"I don't know. Let's kiss and find out."

"If the cameras were rolling, it would be time for a slap right now," she muttered.

He caught her wrist and tugged her closer.

"This isn't a movie, and you're no actor!" she objected.

"Great, because I intend to kiss you for real."

* * *

Hollywood Baby Affair is part of the
Serenghetti Brothers series:
In business and the bedroom,
these alpha brothers drive a hard bargain!

Dear Reader,

I'm thrilled this is the second book about the Serenghetti Brothers—four powerful, passionate Italian American siblings! I've always wanted to write about Hollywood, actresses, scandals and paparazzi.

Actress Chiara Feran needs to distract the press from pesky stories about her gambling-addicted father. Her manager's solution is to set up a sham relationship with Rick Serenghetti. Rick turns out to be more than Chiara bargained for, but she's been on her own too long to think she needs the protection of any man. When Chiara becomes pregnant and then a fan gets too close, will Rick be able to prove to his favorite actress that they are meant to be together?

Watch out for more stories about the Serenghettis, coming soon from Harlequin Desire!

Warmest wishes,

Anna

Website: www.AnnaDePalo.com

Facebook: www.Facebook.com/AnnaDePaloBooks

Twitter: www.Twitter.com/Anna_DePalo

ANNA DePALO

HOLLYWOOD BABY AFFAIR

PAPL
DISCARDED

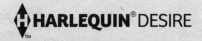 HARLEQUIN® DESIRE

Recycling programs
for this product may
not exist in your area.

ISBN-13: 978-0-373-83852-3

Hollywood Baby Affair

Printed in U.S.A.

HARLEQUIN®
www.Harlequin.com

USA TODAY bestselling author **Anna DePalo** is a Harvard graduate and former intellectual property attorney who lives with her husband, son and daughter in her native New York. She writes sexy, humorous books that have been published in more than twenty countries. Her novels have won the *RT Book Reviews* Reviewers' Choice Award, the Golden Leaf and the Book Buyer's Best. You can sign up for her newsletter at www.annadepalo.com.

Books by Anna DePalo

Harlequin Desire

Having the Tycoon's Baby
Under the Tycoon's Protection
Tycoon Takes Revenge
Cause for Scandal
Captivated by the Tycoon
An Improper Affair
Millionaire's Wedding Revenge
CEO's Marriage Seduction
The Billionaire in Penthouse B
His Black Sheep Bride
One Night with Prince Charming
Improperly Wed

The Serenghetti Brothers

Second Chance with the CEO
Hollywood Baby Affair

Visit her Author Profile page at Harlequin.com, or annadepalo.com, for more titles.

For DeLilah & Bob,
thanks for the support & encouragement

One

Actress and Stuntman Lovefest! More Than Movie Pyrotechnics on Display.

The gossip website headline ran through Chiara Feran's head when it shouldn't have.

She clung to Stunt Stud's well-muscled shoulders, four stories up, wind blowing and helicopter blades whipping in the background—trying to act as if her life depended on it when the truth was that only her career did. After all, a gossip site had just written that she and Mr. Stunt Double were an item, and right now she needed the press distracted from her estranged father, a Vegas-loving cardsharp threatening to cause a controversy of his own.

She tossed her head to keep the hair out of her face. She'd learned Stunt Stud's first name was Rick when they'd rehearsed, but she thought *insufferable* was a better word for him. He had remarkable green eyes…and he looked at her as if she were a spoiled diva who needed the kid-glove treatment.

I don't want you to ruin your manicure.

Thanks for your concern, but there's a manicurist on set.

They'd had a few brief exchanges over the course of filming that had made her blood boil. If the world only knew… True, his magnetism was enough to rival that of the biggest movie stars, so she wondered why he was content with stunt work, but then again, his ego didn't need any further boosting. And the rumors were that he wasn't who he seemed to be and that he had a shadowy, secretive past.

There was even a hint that he was fabulously wealthy. Given his ego, she wouldn't be surprised if he'd put out the rumors himself. He was a macho stuntman ready to save a damsel in distress, but Chiara could save herself, thank you. She'd learned long ago not to depend on any man.

She opened her mouth, but instead of an existential scream, her next line came out. "Zain, we're going to die!"

"I'm not dropping you," he growled in reply.

Chiara knew his voice would be substituted later with her costar's by the studio's editing department. She took perverse satisfaction in calling him by her costar's character name. And since Rick was pretending to be her costar, and her costar himself was just acting, she was two steps removed from reality.

And one long fall away from sudden death.

Even though both she and Rick had invisible harnesses, accidents could and did happen on movie sets. As if on cue, more explosions sounded around them.

As soon as this scene was over, she was heading to her trailer for coffee and maybe even a talk with Odele—

"Cut!" the director yelled through a bullhorn.

Chiara sagged with relief.

Rick barely loosened his grip as they were lowered to the ground.

She was bone-tired in the middle of a twelve-hour day on set. She didn't dwell on the other type of tired right now—an existential weariness that made it hard to care about anything in her life. Fortunately filming on this movie was due to wrap soon.

Action flicks bored her, but they paid the mortgage and more. And Odele, her manager, never stopped reminding her that they also kept her in the public eye. Her Q score would stay high, and it would keep those lucrative endorsement deals flowing. This film was no exception on both counts. *Pegasus Pride* was about a mission to stop the bad guys from blowing up the United Nations and other key government buildings.

As soon as her feet hit the ground, she ignored a frisson of awareness and stepped away from Rick.

His dark hair was mussed, and his jeans clung low on his hips, a dirty vest concealing his tee. Still, he managed to project the authority of a master of the universe, calm and implacable but ready for action.

She didn't like her reaction to him. He made her self-conscious about being a woman. Yes, he was all hard-packed muscle and latent strength. Yes, he was undoubtedly in top physical shape with washboard abs. But he was arrogant and annoying and, like most men, not to be trusted.

She refused to be intimidated. It was laughable really—after all, *her* bank account must dwarf his.

"Okay?" Rick asked.

His voice was as deep and rich as the hot chocolate she wished she had right now—damn him. It was a surprisingly damp and cold early April day on Novatus Studio's lot in Los Angeles. "Of course. Why wouldn't I be?" Dozens of people milled around them on the movie set. "All in a day's work, right?"

His jaw firmed. "This one is asking for more than usual."

"Excuse me?"

He looked at her quizzically. "Have you spoken to your manager recently? Odele?"

"No, why?"

His gaze moved to her trailer. "You may want to give it a go."

Uh-oh.

He fished his cell phone out of his pocket and showed her the screen.

It took a moment to focus on the newspaper website's headline, but once she did, her eyes widened. Chiara Feran and Her Stuntman Get Cozy. Is It More Than High Altitudes That Have Their Hearts Racing?

Oh…crap. Another online tabloid had apparently

picked up the original gossip site's story, and worse, now Rick was aware of it, too. Heat rushed to her cheeks. He wasn't *her* stuntman. He wasn't her anything. Suddenly she wondered whether she should have sent that first story into internet oblivion when she'd had the chance by denying it. But she'd been too relieved they were focusing on a made-up relationship rather than the real pesky issue—her father.

At Rick's amused look, she said abruptly, "I'll talk to Odele."

He lifted her chin and stroked her jaw with his thumb—as if he had all the right in the world. "If you want me, there's no need for extreme measures like planting stories in the press. Why not try the direct approach?"

She swatted his hand away and held on to her temper. "I'm sure there's been a mistake. Is that direct enough for you?"

He laughed at her with his eyes, and said with lazy self-assurance, "Get back to me."

As if. In addition to her deadbeat father making news, she had to contend with burgeoning rumors of a relationship with the last stuntman on earth she'd ever walk the red carpet with.

She turned her back on Rick and marched off. The man sent a red mist into the edges of her vision, and it had nothing to do with lust. She clenched her hands, heart pounding. Her jeans and torn tee were skintight—requisite attire for an action movie damsel in distress—and she was aware she was giving Rick a good view as she stomped away.

At her trailer, she banged through the door. She immediately spotted Odele sitting at a small table. The older woman lifted her head and gave Chiara a mild look from behind red glasses, her gray bob catching the light. If Chiara had learned anything during her years with her manager, it was that Odele was unflappable.

Stopping, Chiara touched her forehead. "I took pain medication for my headache an hour ago, and he's still here."

"Man problems have defied pharmacology for decades, honey," Odele replied in her throaty, raspy voice.

Chiara blurted out the gossip about her and Rick, and the stuntman's reaction. "He thinks he's God's gift to actresses!"

"You need a boyfriend," Odele responded cryptically.

For a moment, Chiara had trouble processing the words. Her mind, going sixty miles an hour, hit the brakes. "What?"

She was one of those actresses who got paid to be photographed sporting a certain brand of handbag or shoes. She glanced around her trailer at the gleaming wood and marble countertops. She had more than she could possibly want. She didn't desire anything, especially a boyfriend.

True, she hadn't had a date in a long time. It didn't mean she couldn't get one. She just didn't want the hassle. Boyfriends were work…and men were trouble.

"We need to retain a boyfriend for you," Odele rephrased.

Chiara gave a dismissive laugh. "I can think of many things I need, but a boyfriend isn't one of them. I need a new stylist now that Emery has gone off to start her own accessories line. I need a new tube of toothpaste for my bathroom. And I really need a vacation once this film wraps." She shook her head. "But a boyfriend? No."

"You're America's sweetheart. Everyone wants to see you happy," her manager pointed out.

"You mean they want to see me making steady progress toward marriage and children."

Odele nodded.

"Life is rarely that neat." She should know.

Odele gave a big sigh. "Well, we don't deal in reality, do we, honey? Our currency in Hollywood is the stardust of dreams."

Chiara resisted rolling her eyes. She *really* needed a vacation.

"That's why a little relationship is just what you need to get your name back out there in a positive way."

"And how am I supposed to get said relationship?"

Odele snapped her fingers. "Easy. I have just the man."

"Who?"

"A stuntman, and you've already met him."

A horrifying thought entered Chiara's head, and she narrowed her eyes. "You put out the rumor that Rick and I are getting cozy."

OMG. She'd gone to Odele with the rumor because she expected her manager to stamp out a budding media firestorm. Instead, she'd discovered Odele was an arsonist…with poor taste in men.

Odele nodded. "Damn straight I did. We need a distraction from stories about your father."

Chiara stepped forward. "Odele, how could you? And with—" she stabbed her finger in the direction of the door "—him of all people."

Odele remained placid.

Chiara narrowed her eyes again. "Has he said anything about your little scheme?"

"He hasn't objected."

No wonder Rick had seemed almost…intimate a few minutes ago. He'd been approached by Odele to be her supposed love interest. Chiara took a deep breath to steady herself and temper her reaction. "He's not my type."

"He's any woman's type, honey. Arm candy."

"There's nothing sweet about him, believe me." He was obnoxious, irritating and objectionable in every way.

"He might not be sugar, but he'll look edible to many of your female fans."

Chiara threw up her hands. It was one thing not to contradict a specious story online, it was another to start pretending it was *true*. And now she'd discovered that said story had been concocted by none other than her own manager. "Oh, c'mon, Odele. You really expect me to stage a relationship for the press?"

Odele arched a brow. "Why not? Your competition is making sex tapes for the media."

"I'm aiming for the Academy Awards, not the Razzies."

"It's no different from being set up on a date or two by a friend."

"Except you're my manager and we both know there's an ulterior motive."

"There's always an ulterior motive. Money. Sex. You name it."

"Is this necessary? My competition has survived extramarital affairs, DUIs and nasty custody disputes with their halos intact."

"Only because of quick thinking and fancy foot-work on the part of their manager or publicist. And believe me, honey, my doctor keeps advising me to keep my stress level to a minimum. It's not good for the blood pressure."

"You need to get out of Hollywood."

"And you need a man. A stuntman."

"Never." And especially not *him*. Somehow he'd gotten his own trailer even though he wasn't one of the leads on this film. He also visited the exercise trailer, complete with built-in gym and weightlifting equipment. Not that she'd used it herself, but his access to it hadn't escaped her notice.

Odele pulled out her cell phone and read from the screen: "Chiara Feran's Father in Illegal Betting Scandal: 'My Daughter Has Cut Me Off.'"

Oh…double damn. Chiara was familiar with yesterday's headline. It was like a bad dream that she kept waking up to. It was also why she'd been temporarily—in a moment of insanity—grateful for the ridiculous story about her budding romance. "The only reason I've kept him out of my life for the past two decades is because he's a lying, cheating snake! Now I'm responsible not only for my own image, but for what a sperm donor does?"

As far as she was concerned, the donation of sperm was Michael Feran's principal contribution to the person she was today. Even the surname that they shared wasn't authentic. It had been changed at Ellis Island three generations back from the Italian *Ferano* to the Anglicized *Feran*.

"We need to promote a wholesome image," Odele intoned solemnly.

"I could throttle him!"

Rick Serenghetti made it his business to be all business. But he couldn't take his gaze off Chiara Feran. Her limpid brown eyes, smooth skin contrasting with dark brows and raven hair made her a dead ringer for Snow White.

A guy could easily be turned into a blithering fool in the presence of such physical perfection. Her face was faultlessly symmetrical. Her topaz eyes called to a man to lose himself in their depths, and her pink bow mouth begged to be kissed. And then came the part of her appearance where the threshold was crossed from fairy tale to his fantasy: she had a fabulous body that marked her as red-hot.

They were in the middle of filming on the Novatus

Studio set. Today was sunny and mild, more typical weather for LA than they'd had yesterday, when he'd last spoken to Chiara. With any luck, current conditions were a bellwether for how filming on the movie would end—quickly and painlessly. Then he could relax, because on a film set he was always pumped up for his next action scene. In a lucky break for everyone involved, scenes were again being shot on Novatus Studio's lot in downtown LA, instead of in nearby Griffith Park.

Still, filming wasn't over until the last scene was done.

He stood off to the side, watching Chiara and the action on camera. The film crew surrounded him, along with everyone else who made a movie happen: assistants, extras, costume designers, special effects people and, of course, the stunts department—*him*.

He knew more about Chiara Feran than she'd ever guess—or that she'd like him to know. No Oscar yet, but the press loved to talk about her. Surprisingly scandal-free for Hollywood...except for the cardsharp father.

Too bad Rick and Chiara rubbed each other like two sheets of sandpaper—because she had guts. He had to respect that about her. She wasn't like her male costar who—if the tabloids were to be believed—was fond of getting four-hundred-dollar haircuts.

At the same time, Chiara was all woman. He remembered the feel of her curves during the helicopter stunt they'd done yesterday. She'd been soft and stimulating. And now the media had tagged him and Chiara as a couple.

"I want to talk to you."

Rick turned to see Chiara's manager. In the first days of filming, he'd spotted the older woman on set. She was hard to overlook. Her raspy, no-nonsense voice and distinctive ruby-framed glasses made her ripe for caricature. One of the crew had confirmed for him that she was Odele Wittnauer, Chiara's manager.

Odele looked to be in her early sixties and not fighting it—which made her stand out in Hollywood. Her helmet hair was salt-and-pepper with an ironclad curve under the chin.

Rick adopted a pleasant smile. He and Odele had exchanged a word or two, but this was the first time she'd had a request. "What can I do for you?"

"I've got a proposal."

He checked his surprise, and joked, "Odele, I didn't think you had it in you."

He had been propositioned by plenty of women, but he'd never had the word *proposal* issue from the mouth of a Madeleine Albright look-alike before.

"Not that type of proposition. I want you to be in a relationship with Chiara Feran."

Rick rubbed his jaw. He hadn't seen that one coming. And then he put two and two together, and a light went off. "You were the one who planted that story about me and Chiara."

"Yup," Odele responded without a trace of guilt or remorse. "The press beast had to be fed. And more important, we needed a distraction from another story about Chiara's father."

"The gambler."

"The deadbeat."

"You're ruthless." He said it with reluctant admiration.

"There's chemistry between you," Odele responded, switching gears.

"Fireworks are more like it."

Chiara's manager brightened. "The press will eat it up. The stuntman and the beauty pageant winner."

So Chiara had won a contest or two—he shouldn't have been surprised. She had the looks to make men weak, including *him*, somewhat to his chagrin. Still, Odele made them sound like a couple on a C-rated reality show: *Blind Date Engagements*. "I've seen the media chew up and spit out people right and left. No, thanks."

"It'll raise your profile in this town."

"I like my privacy."

"I'll pay you well."

"I don't need the money."

"Well," Odele drawled, lowering her eyes, "maybe I can appeal to your sense of stuntman chivalry then."

"What do you mean?"

Odele looked up. "You see, Chiara has this teeny-weeny problem of an overly enthusiastic fan."

"A stalker?"

"Too early to tell, but the guy did try to scale the fence at her house once."

"He knows where she lives?" Rick asked in disbelief.

"We live in the internet age, dear. Privacy is dead."

He had some shred left but he wasn't going to go into details. Even Superman's alter ego, Clark Kent, was entitled to a few secrets.

"Don't mention the too-eager fan to her, though. She doesn't like to talk about it."

Rick narrowed his eyes. "Does Chiara Feran know you approached me?"

"She thinks I already have."

All right then.

He surmised that Odele and Chiara had had their talk. And apparently Chiara had changed tactics and decided to turn the situation to her advantage. She was willing to tolerate him…for the sake of her career at least. He shouldn't have been surprised. He'd already had one bad experience with a publicity-hungry actress, and then he'd been one of the casualties.

Still, they were in the middle of the second act, and he'd missed the opening. But suddenly things had gotten a lot more interesting.

Odele's eyes gleamed as if she sensed victory—or at least a chink in his armor. Turning away, she said, "Let me know when you're ready to talk."

As Rick watched Chiara's manager leave, he knew there was a brooding expression on his face. Odele had presented him with a quandary. As a rule, he didn't get involved with actresses—ever since his one bad episode—but he had his gallant side. On top of it, Chiara was the talent on his latest film—one in which he had a big stake.

As if on cue, his cell phone vibrated. Fishing it out of his pocket, Rick recognized the number on-screen as that of his business partner—one of the guys who fronted the company, per Rick's preference to be behind the scenes.

"Hey, Pete, what's going on?"

Rick listened to Pete's summary of the meeting that morning with an indie director looking for funding. He liked what he heard, but he needed to know more. "Email me their proposal. I'm inclined to fund up to five million, but I want more details."

Five million dollars was pocket change in his world.

"You're the boss," Pete responded cheerfully.

Yup, he was…though no one on set knew he was the producer of *Pegasus Pride*. He liked his privacy and kept his communications mostly to a need-to-know basis.

Right. Rick spotted Chiara in the distance. No doubt she was heading to film her next scene. *There* was someone who treated him more like the hired help than the boss.

Complications and delays on a film were common, and Rick had a feeling Chiara was about to become his biggest complication to date…

Two

"Hey."

It was exactly the sort of greeting she expected from a sweaty and earthy he-man—or rather, stunt-man.

Chiara's pulse picked up. *Ugh.* She hadn't expected to have this reaction around him. She was a professional—a classically trained actress before she'd been diverted by Hollywood.

Sure, she'd been Miss Rhode Island, and a runner-up in the Miss America pageant. But then the Yale School of Drama had beckoned. And she'd never been a Hollywood blonde. The media most often compared her to Camilla Belle because they shared a raven-haired, chestnut-eyed look.

Anyway, with her ebony hair, she'd need to have

her roots touched up every other day if she tried to become a blonde. As far as she was concerned, she spent enough time in the primping chair.

She figured He-Stuntman had gotten his education in the School of Hard Knocks. Maybe a broken bone or two. Certainly plenty of bumps and bruises.

Rick stopped in front of her. No one was around. They were near the actors' trailers, far away from the main action. Luckily she hadn't run into him after her talk with Odele two days ago. Instead, she'd managed to avoid him until now.

Dusk was gathering, but she still had a clear view of him.

He was in a ripped tee, jeans and body paint meant to seem like grease and dirt, while she was wearing a damsel-in-distress/sidekick look—basically a feminine version of Rick's attire but her clothes were extratight and torn to show cleavage. And from the quick perusal he gave her, she could tell the bare skin hadn't escaped his notice.

"So you need a boyfriend," he said without preamble.

She itched to rub the smug smile off his face. "I don't need anything. This would be a completely optional but mutually advantageous arrangement."

And right after this conversation, she was going to have another serious talk with her manager. What had Odele signed her up for?

"You need me."

She burned. He'd made it sound like *you want me*.

"I've been asked to play many roles, but never a stud."

"Don't get too excited."

He grinned. "Don't worry, I won't. I have a thing for the doe-eyed, dark-haired look, but since Camilla Belle isn't available, you'll do."

The flames of temper licked her, not least because he was clued in as to her Hollywood doppelgänger. "So you'll settle?"

"I don't know. Let's kiss and find out."

"If the cameras were rolling, it would be time for a slap right now," she muttered.

He caught her wrist and tugged her closer.

"This isn't a movie, and you're no actor!" she objected.

"Great, because I intend to kiss you for real. Let's see if we can be convincing for when the paparazzi and public are watching." He raised his free hand to thread his fingers through her hair and move it away from her face. "Your long dark hair is driving me crazy."

"It's the Brazilian-Italian heritage," she snapped back, "and I bet you say the same thing to all your leading ladies."

"No," he answered bemusedly, "some of them are blondes."

And then his mouth was on hers. If he'd been forceful, she'd have had a chance, but his lips settled on hers with soft, tantalizing pressure. He smelled of smoke from the special effects, and when his tongue slipped inside her mouth, she discovered the taste of mint, too.

She'd been kissed many times—on-screen and off—but she found herself tumbling into this one with shocking speed. The kiss was smooth, leisurely… masterful but understated. Rick could double for any A-list actor in a love scene. He touched his tongue to hers, and the shock and unexpectedness of it had her opening to him. As an unwritten rule, actors on-screen did not French kiss, so she was already in uncharted territory. The hard plane of his chest brushed against her, and her nipples tightened.

Think, Chiara. Remember why you don't like him.

She allowed herself one more second, and then she tore her mouth away and stepped back. For a fleeting moment she felt a puff of steam over his audacity. "All right, the screen test is over."

Rick curved his lips. "How did I do?"

"I don't even know your last name," she responded, sidestepping the question.

"I'll answer to anything. 'Honey,' 'baby,' 'sugar.'" He shrugged. "I'm easy."

"Clearly." This guy could charm his way into any woman's bed. "Still, I'd prefer your real one for when the police ask me to describe the suspect."

He grinned. "It's Rick Serenghetti. But 'darling' would add the appropriate air of mystery for the paparazzi."

Serenghetti. She knew an Italian surname when she heard one. "My last name was originally Ferano. You know, Italian."

His smile widened. "I'd never have guessed, Snow White."

"They used to call me Snow White, but I drifted," she quipped. "Not suitable for the role."

"No problem. I'm not Prince Charming. I'm just his body double."

She wanted to scream. "This is never going to work."

"That's why you're an actress." He looked curious. "And, Odele mentioned, a beauty contestant. Win any titles?"

She made a sour face. "Yes. Miss Congeniality."

He burst out laughing. "I won't ask what your talent was."

"Ventriloquism. I made my dummy sing."

"'Some Day My Prince Will Come'?"

"Nothing from *Snow White*! I was also Miss Rhode Island, but obviously that was on the state level." She'd gone on to be a finalist in Miss America, which was where she'd earned her title of Miss Congeniality.

"Rhode Island is the smallest state. Still, the competition must have been fierce."

"Are you mocking me?" She searched his face, but he looked solemn.

"Who, me? I never mock women I'm trying to score with."

"Wow, you're direct. You don't even like me."

"What's *like* got to do with it?"

"You have no shame." When it came to sex, she

was used to men wanting to bed anyone in sight. This was Hollywood, after all.

"Is it working?"

"Nothing will work, except Odele convincing me this is a good idea."

Rick frowned. "You mean she hasn't already?"

It took Chiara a moment to realize he wasn't joking. "Please. She may have persuaded you to go along with her crazy scheme, but not me."

"I only went along with it because I thought you'd said yes."

Chiara watched Rick's dawning expression, which mimicked her own. "I believed you'd agreed."

"Stuntmen are made of sterner stuff." He threw her attitude right back at her.

Chiara realized they'd both been tricked by Odele into believing the other had agreed to her plan. Rick had dared to kiss her because he thought she'd already signed up for her manager's plot. "What are we going to do?"

Rick shrugged. "About the gathering media frenzy? We're already bickering like an old married couple. We're perfect."

Chiara's eyes widened. "You can't tell me you're seriously considering this? Anyway, we're supposed to act like new lovebirds, not a cantankerous old married couple."

"If we're already arguing, it'll make our relationship seem deeper than it is."

"Skip the honeymoon phase?" she asked rhetorically. "What's in this for you?"

He shrugged. "Have some fun." He looked at her lingeringly. "Satisfy my fetish for Snow White."

Chiara tingled, her breasts feeling heavy. "Oh, yeah, right..."

"So what's your take?"

"This is the worst storyline to come out of Hollywood."

For the second time in recent days, Chiara banged open the door of her trailer and marched in. "I can't pretend to be in a relationship with Rick Serenghetti. End of story."

Odele looked up from her magazine. She sat on a cushioned built-in bench along one wall. "What's wrong with him?"

He was too big, too macho, too everything—most of all, *annoying.* She still sizzled from their kiss minutes ago, and she didn't do vulnerability where men were concerned. But she sidestepped the issue. "It's the pretending part that I have trouble with."

"You're an actress."

"Context is everything. I like to confine my acting to the screen." Otherwise, she'd be in danger of losing herself. If she was always pretending, who was she? "You know I value integrity."

"It's overrated. Besides, this is Tinseltown."

Chiara placed her hands on her hips. "You misled me and Rick into thinking the other one had already agreed to this crazy scheme."

Odele shrugged. "You were already open to the

idea. That's the only reason it even mattered to you whether he was already on board with the plan."

Chiara felt heat rise to her face, and schooled her expression. "I'm not signing up for anything!"

Her conversation with Rick had had no satisfactory ending. It had sent her scuttling, somewhat humiliatingly, back to her manager. Chiara eyed the shower stall visible through the open bathroom door at the end of the trailer. If only she could rinse off the tabloid headlines just as easily.

"Fine," Odele responded with sudden and suspicious docility, putting aside her magazine. "We'll have to come up with another strategy to distract the press from your father and amp up your career."

"Sounds like a plan to me."

"Great, it's settled. Now…can you gain twenty pounds?" Odele asked.

Chiara sighed. Out of the frying pan and into the fire. "I'd rather not. Why?"

She'd gained fifteen for a film role two years ago in *Alibis & Lies*—in which she'd played a convicted white-collar criminal who witnesses a murder once she's released from jail and thinks her husband is framing her. To gain the weight, she'd indulged her love for pasta, creamy sauces and pastries—but she'd had to work for months with a trainer to shed the pounds afterward. In the meantime, she'd worn sunglasses and baggy clothes and had lain low in order to avoid an unflattering shot by the paparazzi. And she'd been disappointed not to get a Golden Globe nomination.

She wondered what movie project Odele had in mind these days… Usually her talent agent at Creative Artists sent projects her way, but Odele kept her ear to the ground, too.

"Last time I was heavier on-screen, I got a lot of backlash." Some fans thought she'd gained too much weight, some too little. She could never please everyone.

"It's not a film," Odele said. "It's a weight-loss commercial."

Chiara's jaw dropped. "But I'm not overweight!"

Odele's eyes gleamed. "You could be."

Chiara threw her hands up. "Odele, you're ruthless."

"It's what makes me good at what I do. Slender You is looking for a new celebrity weight-loss spokesperson. The goodwill with fans alone is worth the pounds, but Slender You is willing to pay millions to the right person. If you land this contract, your DBI score will go up, and you'll be more likely to land other endorsement deals."

"No." Her manager was all about Q scores and DBIs and any other rating that claimed to measure a celebrity's appeal to the public. "Next you'll be suggesting a reality show."

Odele shook her head. "No, I only recommend it to clients who haven't had a big acting job in at least five years. That's not you, sweetie."

For which Chiara would be forever grateful. She was having a hard enough time being the star of her own life without adding the artifice of a reality show to it.

"How about writing a book?" Odele asked, tilting her head.

"On what?"

"Anything! We'll let your ghostwriter decide."

"No, thanks. If I have a ghost, I won't really be writing, will I?" Chiara responded tartly.

"You're too honest for your own good, you know." Odele sighed, and then suddenly brightened. "What about a fragrance?"

"I thought Dior just picked a new face for the brand."

"They did. I'm talking about developing your own scent. Very lucrative these days."

"You mean like Elizabeth Taylor's White Diamonds?"

"Right, right." Odele warmed up. "We could call it Chiara. Or, wait, wait, Chiara Lucida! The name suggests a bright star."

"How much is an Oscar worth?" Chiara joked, because her idea of becoming a big star involved winning a golden statuette.

"Of course, an Academy Award has value, but we want to monetize all income streams, sweetie. We want to grow and protect your brand."

Chiara sighed, leaning against the walnut-paneled built-in cabinet behind her. There'd been a time when movie stars were just, well, movie stars. Now everyone was *a brand*. "There's nothing wrong with my brand."

"Yes, of course." Odele paused for a beat. "Well, except for the teeny-weeny problem of your father popping up in the headlines from time to time."

"Right." How could she forget? How could anyone fail to remember when the tabloids followed the story breathlessly?

"How about a lifestyle brand like Gwyneth Paltrow or Jessica Alba has?" Odele offered.

"Maybe when I win an Academy Award or I have kids." Both Alba and Paltrow had had children when they'd started their companies.

At the thought of kids, Chiara had an uncomfortable feeling in the pit of her stomach. She was thirty-two. She had an expiration date in Hollywood *and* a ticking clock for getting pregnant without spending thousands of dollars for chancy medical intervention. Unfortunately the two trains were on a collision course. If she was going to avert disaster, she needed to have a well-established career—er, Oscar—before she caved in to the public clamor for her to get a happily-ever-after with marriage and children.

Of course, she wanted kids. It was the husband or boyfriend part that she had a problem with. Michael Feran hadn't set a sterling example for his only child. At least she thought she was his only child.

Ugh. Her family—or what remained of it—was so complicated. It wouldn't even qualify as a Lifetime movie because there was no happy ending.

Still, the thought of a child of her own brought a pang. She'd have someone to love unconditionally, and who would love and need her in return. She'd avoid the mistakes that her parents had made. And she'd have something real—pure love—to hold on to in the maelstrom of celebrity.

"So," Odele said pleasantly, "your other options aren't too appealing. Let me know when you're ready to consider dating Rick Serenghetti."

Chiara stared at her manager. She had the sneaking suspicion that Odele had known all along where their conversation was heading. In all probability, her manager had been set on showing her the error of her ways and her earlier agreeableness had just been a feint. "You're a shark, Odele."

Odele chuckled. "I know. It's why I'm good at what I do."

Chiara resisted throwing up her hands. Some actresses confided in their personal assistants or stylists. She had Odele.

"So what's got you down?"

Rick figured he needed to work on his acting skills if even Jordan was asking that question. "I don't know what you're talking about."

They were sitting in his kitchen, and he'd just handed his brother a cold beer from the fridge. He grabbed opportunities with his family whenever he could since he spent much of his time on the opposite coast from everyone else. Fortunately, since his current movie was being filmed on a Novatus Studio lot and nearby locations around LA, he was able to get to his place at least on weekends—even if home these days was a one-bedroom rental in West Hollywood.

"Mom asked me to check on you." Jordan shifted his weight on the kitchen barstool.

"She always asks you to check on me whenever we're in the same city. But don't assume the reconnaissance runs one way. She wants me to keep an eye on you, too."

"My life hasn't been that interesting lately."

Jordan was in town because his team, the New England Razors, was playing the Los Angeles Kings at the Staples Center. He was the star center player for the team. The youngest Serenghetti brother also had movie star looks, and hardly ever let an opportunity pass without remarking that their parents had attained perfection the third time around.

Rick followed hockey—family loyalty and all—but he wasn't passionate about it like Jordan and their older brother, Cole, who'd also had a career with the Razors until it had ended in injury. Rick had been a wrestler in high school, not a hockey team captain like his brothers.

The result was that he had a reputation as the family maverick. And hey, who was he to argue? Still, he wasn't intentionally contrary—though Chiara might want to argue the point.

An image of Chiara Feran sprung to mind. He'd been willing to tease her about playing a couple, especially when he'd thought Chiara was going along with the idea. After all, it was nice, safe, *pretend*—not like really getting involved with an actress. And it was fun to ruffle Chiara's feathers.

If he was being a little more serious, he'd also ac-

knowledge that as a producer, he had a vested interest in the star of his latest film maintaining a positive
public image despite her problematic family mem-
bers—not to mention staying *safe* if she really had a
would-be stalker.

Still, being a *pretend boyfriend* and *secret bodyguard*, if Odele had her way, was asking a lot. Did
he have enough to overcome his scruples about getting involved with a celebrity? Hell, even he wasn't
sure. He'd been burned once by an aspiring starlet,
and he'd learned his lesson—never stand between an
actress and a camera.

For a long time, he'd counted actors, directors and
other movie people among his friends. Hal Moldado,
a lighting technician, had been one of those buddies.
Then one day, Rick had run into Isabel Lanier, Hal's
latest girlfriend. She'd followed him out of a cafe
and surprised him with a kiss—captured in a selfie
that she'd managed to take with her cell phone and
promptly posted to her social media accounts. Un-
surprisingly it had spelled the end of his friendship
with Hal. Later he'd conclude that Isabel had just been
trying to make Hal jealous and stay in the news herself as an actress.

The saving grace had been that the media had
never found out—or cared—about the name of Isabel's mystery man in those photos. It had been enough
that Isabel looked as if she were cheating on Hal, so
Rick had been able to dodge the media frenzy.

Ever since, though, as far as he was concerned,
starlets were only interested in tending their public

image. And up to now Chiara had fit the bill well—even if she hadn't yet agreed to her manager's latest scheme. After all, there was a reason that Chiara had partnered with someone like Odele. She knew her celebrity was important, and she needed someone to curate it.

But Odele had increased the stakes by referring to a possible stalker... It complicated his calculations about whether to get involved. He should just convince Chiara to get additional security—like any sane person would. Not that *sanity* ranked high on the list of characteristics he associated with fame-hungry actresses.

Jordan tilted his head. "Woman in your thoughts?"

Rick brought his attention back to the present. "Anyone ever tell you that you have a sixth sense where the other sex is concerned?"

His younger brother smiled enigmatically. "Sera would agree with you. Marisa's cousin is driving me crazy."

Their brother Cole had recently married the love of his life, Marisa Danieli. The two had had a falling-out in high school but had reconnected. Marisa's relatives were now an extension by marriage of the Serenghetti clan—including Marisa's younger cousin Sera.

Apparently that didn't sit well with Jordan.

"I'm surprised," Rick remarked. "You can usually charm any woman if you set your mind to it."

"She won't even serve me at the Puck & Shoot."

"Is she still moonlighting as a waitress there?"

Rick had had his share of drinks at Welsdale's local sports bar.

"Off and on."

He clasped his brother's shoulder. "So your legendary prowess with women has fallen short. Cheer up, it was bound to happen sometime."

"Your support is overwhelming," Jordan replied drily.

Rick laughed. "I just wish Cole were here to appreciate this."

"For the record, I haven't been trying to score with Sera. She's practically family. But she actively dislikes me, and I can't figure out why."

"Why does it matter? It won't be the first time a family member has had it in for you." Jordan had come in for his share of ribbing and roughing up by his two older siblings. "What's to get worked up about?"

"I'm not worked up," Jordan grumbled. "Anyway, let's get back to you and the woman problems."

Rick cracked a careless smile. "Unlike you, I don't have any."

"Women or problems?"

"Both together."

Jordan eyed him. "The press is suggesting you have the former, and you look as if you've got the latter."

"Oh, yeah?"

"Who's the starlet on your latest film?"

"Chiara Feran."

His brother nodded. "She's hot."

"She's off-limits."

Jordan raised his eyebrows. "To me?"

"To anyone."

"Proprietary already?"

"Where did you get this ridiculous story?"

"Hey, I read."

"Much to Mom's belated joy."

Jordan flashed the famous pearly whites. His good looks had gotten him many modeling gigs, including more than one underwear ad. "*Gossipmonger* reported you two have been getting cozy, and the story has been picked up by other websites."

"You know better than to believe everything you read." If the gossip had reached Jordan, then it was spreading wider and faster than Rick had thought. Still, he figured he shouldn't have been surprised, considering Chiara's celebrity.

"Yup. But is it true?"

Frankly, Rick was starting not to know what was true anymore, and it was troubling. "Nothing's happened."

Except one kiss. She'd tasted of peaches—fruity and heady and delicious. He'd gotten an immediate image of the two of them heating up the sheets, his trailer or hers. She challenged him, and something told him she'd be far from boring in bed, too. Chiara was full of fire, and he warmed up immediately around her. The trouble was he might also get burned.

Jordan studied him. "So nothing's happened yet…"

Rick adopted a bland expression. "Unlike you, I don't see women as an opportunity."

"Only your female stars."

"I'm done with that." Isabel had been the star of Rick's movie when they'd been snapped together. The fact that they'd both been working on the film—he as a stuntman and secretly as a producer, and she as an actress—had lent an air of truth to the rumors.

Jordan looked thoughtful. "Right."

Rick checked his watch because he was through trying to convince his brother—or himself. In a quarter of an hour, they needed to head to dinner at Ink, one of the neighborhood's trendy restaurants. "Just finish your damn beer."

"Whatever you say, movie star," Jordan responded, seemingly content to back off.

They both took a swill of their beers.

"So, the new digs treating you well?" his brother asked after a moment.

The apartment had come furnished, so there wasn't a hint of his personality here, but it served its purpose. "The house is nearly done. I'll be moving in a few weeks."

Jordan saluted him with his beer bottle. "Here's to moving up in the world in a big way." His brother grinned. "Invite me to visit when the new manse is done."

"Don't worry. I'll tell the majordomo not to throw you out," Rick replied drily.

Jordan laughed. "I'm a babe magnet. You'll want me around."

Privately, Rick acknowledged his brother might have a point. These days, the only woman he was linked to was Chiara Feran, and it wasn't even real.

Three

For two days, Rick didn't encounter Chiara. She and Adrian Collins, the male lead, were busy filming, so today Rick was hitting the gym trailer and working off restless energy.

So far, there'd been no denial or affirmation in the press that he and Chiara were a couple. As a news story, they were stuck in limbo—a holding pattern that kept him antsy and out of sorts. He wondered what Chiara's camp was up to, and then shrugged. He wasn't going to call attention to himself by issuing a denial—not that the press cared about his opinion because for all they knew, he was just a stuntman. They were after Chiara.

After exiting the gym trailer, Rick made his way across the film set. He automatically tensed as he neared Chiara's trailer. Snow White was a tart-tongued irritant these days—

He rounded a corner and spotted a man struggling with the knob on Chiara's door.

The balding guy with a paunch was muttering to himself and jiggling the door hard.

Frowning, Rick moved toward him. This section of the set was otherwise deserted.

"Hey," he called, "what are you doing?"

The guy looked up nervously.

All Rick's instincts told him this wasn't a good situation. "What are you doing?"

"I'm a friend of Chiara's."

"Does she know you're here?"

"I've been trying to see her." This time there was a note of whininess.

"This is a closed set. Do you have ID?" Rick didn't recall seeing this guy before. He was within a few feet of the other man now. The guy stood on the top step leading to the door of the trailer. Rick could see perspiration had formed on the man's brow. Was this the creepy fan Odele had referred to?

Rick went with his gut. "I'm her new boyfriend."

The other guy frowned. "That's impossible."

Now that he was closer, Rick could see the other man was definitely not the glamorous or debonair celebrity type that he would expect an actress like Chiara to date.

In the next second, the guy barreled down the trailer's steps and shoved past him.

Rick staggered but grasped the trailer's flimsy metal bannister to keep himself upright.

As Chiara's alleged friend made a run for it, Rick instinctively took off after him.

The man plowed past a crew member, who careened back against a piece of lighting equipment. Then two extras jumped aside, creating a path for the chase.

The guy headed toward the front gate of the studio lot, where Rick knew security would stop him. Rick could only guess how the intruder had gotten onto the lot. Had he hidden in the back of a catering truck, as paparazzi had been known to do?

Gaining on Chiara's admirer, Rick put on a final burst of speed and tackled the guy. As they both went down, Rick saw in his peripheral vision that they'd attracted the security guards' attention at the front gate.

The man struggled in his grasp, jabbing Rick with his elbow. "Get off me! I'll sue you for assault."

Rick twisted the man's arm behind his back, holding him down. "Not before you get written up for trespassing. Where's your pass?"

"I'm Chiara's fiancé," the guy howled.

Rick glanced up to see that two security guards had caught up to them. "I found this guy trying to break into Chiara Feran's trailer."

"Call Chiara," her alleged fiancé puffed. "She'll know."

"Chiara Feran doesn't have a fiancé," Rick bit back.

Someone nearby had started filming with his cell phone. *Great.*

"We're together. We're meant to be together!"

Nut job. Rick was in great physical shape due to his stunt work, so he wasn't out of breath, but Mr. Fiancé was no teddy bear, either; he continued to put up a struggle.

Suddenly the trespasser wheezed. "I can't br-breathe! Get off me. I have asthma."

Great. Rick eased back and let one of the security guards take over while the other spoke into his radio.

Things happened slowly but methodically after that. Police were summoned by the studio's security, and Chiara's special fan—who'd given his name as Todd Jeffers—was led away. Eventually Rick was questioned by a police officer. Chiara materialized soon after and was similarly prodded for details by the officer's partner.

Before the police left, Rick gleaned that Chiara's overly enthusiastic fan would be charged with criminal trespass, disorderly conduct and harassment. *Well, that's something.* But by the time Rick had finished talking about the incident to Dan, the director, Chiara had holed up in her trailer.

Rick eyed Chiara's door, twisted his mouth in a grim line and made his way to the trailer for some answers.

He didn't bother knocking—chances were better for a snowstorm in LA right now than for her rolling out the red carpet for him—and simply marched inside.

He came up short when he found Chiara sitting at a cozy little table, a script in front of her.

She was memorizing her lines? He expected her to be rattled, upset…

He looked around. The trailer was a double-decker, and with walnut paneling, it was swankier than his own digs, which were done in a gray monochrome and had no upper level.

When his gaze came back to rest on Chiara, she tilted her head, and said, "People weren't sure when you tackled him whether it was a stunt, or if you were rehearsing a scene from the movie."

"You're welcome." Leaning against a counter, he folded his arms, like a cop getting ready for an interrogation. He wanted answers only she could provide, and after getting into a fight with her admirer, he was going to get them. "Luckily you weren't in your trailer when he got here."

"I was rehearsing. We're shooting a difficult scene."

Rick figured that helped explain why she was sitting with a script in front of her, though he imagined her concentration was shot.

"I can only imagine the press coverage that today will get." A horrified look crossed her face, and she closed her eyes on a shudder.

So she wasn't as unaffected as she seemed. In fact, Rick had already dealt with suppressing the video of him tackling Jeffers. The person who'd been taping had turned out to be a visiting relative of one of the film crew. But even if those images didn't become public or weren't sold to the tabloids, the media would get wind of what happened from the police report and show up for Jeffers's court hearing. Then, of course, Jeffers himself might choose to make a public statement…

"Hey, at least it'll take attention away from your father's latest losses at the gambling tables." He wondered if Chiara appreciated just how close she'd come to danger. It had been dumb luck that her overly enthusiastic fan hadn't found her earlier.

She opened her eyes and raised her head. "Yes, how can I forget about my father? How can anyone?"

"So you have a stalker." He kept his tone mild, belying the emotions coursing through him. *Damn it.* Chiara was slender and a lightweight despite her mouth and bravado. His blood boiled just thinking of some jerk threatening her.

"Many celebrities have overly enthusiastic fans." She waved her hand, and Rick could practically see her walls going up. "But my property has a security gate and cameras."

Rick narrowed his eyes. "Have you dealt with this Todd Jeffers guy before? What kind of unstoppable fan is he? The sort who writes you pretty letters or the type who pens twisted ones?"

She shrugged. "He tried to scale my property fence once, but he was spotted by a landscaper and shooed away even before he got within view of the security cameras. I haven't heard from him in the months since."

So today's guy was the same person who'd shown up at Chiara's house once, and yeah, she wasn't understanding the risk… Still, Rick strove for patience.

"How do you know it was Jeffers at your house that day?"

She hesitated. "He wrote to me afterward to say he'd tried to see me."

"He wrote to you about an attempted criminal trespass?" Rick let his tone drip disbelief. "Have you gotten a temporary restraining order?"

Chiara sighed. "No. He's never been a physical threat, just a pest."

"Just because he *only* tried to jump the fence doesn't mean that's what he'll settle for doing in the future. There's often an escalation with these nut jobs once they figure out that plan A isn't working."

Chiara raised her chin. "He's probably a lonely, starstruck guy. Plenty of fans are."

"Probably? I don't deal in probabilities. Your run-of-the-mill serial killer often starts out torturing animals before moving to the big time. As I said, escalation."

"Like A-list stars starting out in B movies?" she asked snippily.

"Right," he said, his voice tight even as he ignored her flippant attitude. "Listen, Snow White, there are villains out there aside from the Evil Queen."

Rick raked his fingers through his hair. He could understand why this guy was besotted with Chiara. Unfortunately Chiara herself wasn't appreciating the gravity of the problem. They were like two trains on parallel tracks. "You've got a stalker. It's time you acquired a boyfriend. Me."

He'd been mulling things over, his mind in overdrive ever since he'd tackled Jeffers. If he pretended to be Chiara's boyfriend, he could stick close and keep an eye on her. Maybe once this guy realized Chiara had a supposedly real boyfriend, he'd back off. Odele may have been onto a good idea.

Chiara opened and closed her mouth. "You're not in the protection business."

"I'm appointing myself right now. Besides, I've got the right background. I used to do security." He'd worked as a guard at an office building during his college days and beyond in order to earn extra cash. He'd been a good bouncer, too. His parents had instilled the value of hard work in their children even though they'd been well-off.

Chiara slid off her seat and stood. In the confined space, she was within touching distance. "You can't unilaterally decide to be my protector." She spluttered as if searching for words. "I won't agree to it."

"You could solve two problems at once. The bad press from your father, and the issue of your stalker and needing security. Don't quibble."

"I'll get a restraining order."

He took a step forward. "Damn straight, you will."

"So I don't need you."

"You need physical protection, too, unless you have seven dwarves hanging around, because a court order is just a piece of paper." He didn't want to think about how many news stories there'd been concerning an order of protection being violated—and someone getting hurt or killed.

She looked mutinous. "I'll hire professional security."

"It still won't solve the problem of your father and distracting the press."

Chiara threw up her hands.

"Don't worry. I'll always be a step behind you, like a good prince consort—I mean, bodyguard."

"Hilarious."

"I'll make sure to hold an umbrella open for you in the rain," he added solemnly.

"What's in this for you?"

"Let's just say I have a vested interest in the star of my next blockbuster staying safe until the end of filming. Everyone working on this movie wants to see it finished so they can get paid."

"I thought so. Well, my answer is still no."

He'd given her the wrong answer, and she'd responded in kind. "Do you just act contrary, or is this your best side?"

"How can you say that about the damsel in distress you helped save from a helicopter?" she asked sweetly.

"Exactly."

They were practically nose-to-nose, except because she stood several inches shorter than his six-foot frame, it was more like nose-to-chin. But then she raised her face to a stubborn angle, and he abandoned his good intentions about keeping himself in check during this conversation.

Hell, here goes nothing.

He tugged her forward and captured her mouth.

It was just as good as before, damn it. There was a little zap of electricity because they were differently charged, and then he was kissing her in earnest, opening that luscious mouth and deepening the kiss.

She smelled faintly of honeysuckle, just like Snow White ought to. He caressed her cheek with the back of his hand. She was petal-soft, and he was getting hard.

After what felt like an eternity, she pushed him away.

Her chest rose and fell, and he was breathing deeply with arousal.

She touched her fingers to her lips and then shot fire at him with her eyes. "That's twice."

"Are we getting better? We've got to be convincing if we're going to pull this off."

"We're not practicing scenes, but if we were, try this response on for size." She stretched out her arm and pointed to the door of the trailer, giving him his marching orders.

It was a proverbial slap in the face, but Chiara was wrong if she thought he was backing down. "Let me know when our next scene is scheduled for filming. It might be time to throw a plate or break something. For real, not pretend."

After this parting shot, he turned and headed to the door, almost laughing as he heard her bang something behind him.

"She doesn't want to get extra security." Rick ran his hand through his hair. "She's stubborn."

"Hmm." Odele nodded. "And I'm her manager, so I don't know this?"

"And reckless, too." They were sitting in Novatus Studio's commissary having coffee before lunchtime. Rick had asked to meet and had told Odele not to mention it to Chiara. "How long has this guy Todd been hanging around thinking he's her special friend?" *Or fiancé.*

Odele shrugged. "Several months. I had staff look at Chiara's fan mail after he showed up at her house. He'd sent an email or two, and my assistant says he's cropped up on social media, too. Then he started a fan club and wanted autographed photos."

"And now he's moved on to believing he's her fiancé."

Odele sighed. "Some people buy into the Hollywood celebrity stuff a little too much."

Right. Rick leaned back in his chair. "Besides trying to scale the fence at Chiara's house, has he made any other moves?"

"Not until yesterday. At least not that I know of." Odele took a sip from her cup. "I've already instructed Chiara's attorney to go for a restraining order."

"You and I both know it's only a piece of paper, but she doesn't want to consider additional physical security. Not even if I appoint myself." Rick didn't hide the frustration in his voice. Damn it. Who was he kidding? Chiara would resist, especially if it was him.

"So you're considering my idea of being a pretend boyfriend? You need to move in."

Rick shook his head in exasperation because Odele

was a bulldozer. "If she doesn't want a fake relationship and won't tolerate a bodyguard, she definitely
won't have someone living in her house."

If he and Chiara lived under one roof, they'd drive
each other crazy. He'd alternate between wanting to
shake some sense into her and take her to bed. And
she'd... Well, she'd just rage at him and deny any
sparks of a simmering attraction.

It was a recipe for disaster...or a Hollywood movie.

Odele gave him a mild look. "It's all a matter of
how it's presented to her. If you're going to distract
the press as her new boyfriend, the story will play
even bigger in the media if you move in. There'll be
more opportunities for the two of you to be photographed together."

"*Pretend* boyfriend." Everyone needed to be clear
on the fake part, including and particularly *him*, if he
was going to get involved with another actress.

Odele inclined her head. "Leave convincing her
to me. I won't say anything more about having you
function as a bodyguard. But believe me, the press attention surrounding her father is really upsetting her."

In Rick's opinion, Chiara should be spending more
time worrying about her stalker than about her estranged father. Still... "Tell me about Michael Feran."

Odele set aside her coffee cup. "There's not much
to say. Chiara's parents divorced when she was young.
Chiara and her mother were in Rhode Island until
Hollywood beckoned. Her mother died a few years
ago. She developed sepsis after an illness. It was a
shock for everyone."

"But her father continues to make waves."

"Last year, he accepted money from a third-rate weekly to dish about Chiara."

Rick cursed.

Odele shot him a perceptive look from behind her red glasses. "Yes, Chiara felt betrayed."

So Chiara's was far from a fairy-tale upbringing. No wonder she was prickly around him, and no doubt distrustful of men.

"Take it from me. Be the good boyfriend that she needs and keep an eye on her. Just don't bring up the bodyguard part to her."

"A pretend boyfriend." *Pretend* being the operative word there. He wasn't sure if he was reminding himself or Odele, though.

"Right."

Right.

Chiara took Ruby out of her box and perched her on her knee. The dummy wore a sequined gown, and her hair and face were worthy of a Vegas showgirl.

Chiara sat at the writing desk occupying one corner of her master bedroom. There'd been a break in filming for the weekend, and she was happy to retreat to her sanctuary. She needed time away. First her father, then Rick and finally a stalker had frayed her nerves.

Still, even though it was a beautiful and sunny Saturday afternoon, and she should have been in a great mood, she…*wasn't*. She was irritable and restless and anxious. She'd been having trouble memorizing her lines ever since the attempted break-in at her trailer. *Pegasus Pride* was an action flick, so the script wasn't heavy, but there was still dialogue that she had to be able to say without prompting.

Frustrated, she'd finally resorted to using Ruby to help her relax. She hadn't taken the dummy out in months, but ventriloquism kept her in touch with her former life—and at moments like these, let her deal with her present concerns.

Chiara searched the dummy's face. "What am I going to do?"

Ruby tilted her head.

"I must be out of my mind to be talking to a dummy by myself."

"You're not alone if you're having a chat with someone," Ruby responded in her singsong voice. "I just help you figure things out, sugar."

"I thought that's what Odele is for."

Ruby waved her hand. "You already know where Odele stands. She's on the hunk's side, and frankly, I don't know why you aren't, too." Ruby tossed her hair—because rolling her eyes was out of the question. "He's delicious."

"Annoying. You're reading too much gossip."

"I have to, it's about you," the dummy chirped. "Anyway, it's time you let someone under your skin, and back into your bed. And Rick…that body, that face, that kiss. Need I say more?"

"You are saucy and naughty, Ruby."

"And you wish you could be. Let your hair down, sugar."

Chiara's gaze fell to the laptop at her elbow. "I have too many responsibilities…and plenty of problems."

The headline on the computer screen spoke for itself: Chiara Feran's Father Thrown Out of Casino.

Maybe now that he couldn't gamble because he'd been caught counting cards, Michael Feran would stay out of trouble. But Chiara knew that was wishful thinking.

The public thought she had an enviable life—helped by Odele's relentless image craftsmanship. But the truth…

She'd never thought of herself as a beauty queen, for one. Oh, sure, she'd been blessed with good genes—a nice face and a fast metabolism that meant it wasn't impossible to adhere to Hollywood standards of beauty. But she also considered herself an outsider. She'd been raised by an immigrant mother, grown up enduring cold New England winters and would have still been doing theater but for a quirk of fate and Odele risking taking her on as a client.

She liked her privacy, her best friend was a smart-mouthed talent manager ripe for caricature and her sidekick was a doll made of wood. Obviously Todd Jeffers was crazier than she gave him credit for if he couldn't pick a better-credentialed starlet to stalk. And now she had a rumored *boyfriend*—a muscle-bound stuntman who looked as if he could enter a triathlon.

She'd already ignored a text from Odele about the latest headline, but Chiara knew her manager was right—they needed a distraction *fast*…

Her lawyers were due in court in the coming days to get a temporary restraining order—so there'd be more unwanted press attention because of her unpleasant fan.

Still, Rick Serenghetti? *Argh.*

Her cell phone buzzed again, a telltale ringtone, and this time Chiara knew she couldn't ignore it. With an apologetic look, she propped Ruby on a chair and took the call. "Hello, Odele."

"Enjoying your time off?"

"Define *enjoy.* I'm memorizing my lines." Among other things. She cast Ruby a hush-hush look.

"Rick needs to move in if we're going to make this fake relationship work. It'll help believability."

"No." The refusal fell from her lips without thought. Rick in her house? They'd throttle each other…if they weren't jumping into bed. And the contradiction of trying to make a *fake* relationship *work* was apparently lost on her manager.

Odele sighed. "We need to move quickly. I'm going to tell my assistant to break the story on social media accounts so we can control the initial message. I took an amateur shot with my cell phone of you and Rick seemingly engaged in an intimate conversation on the Novatus Studio lot."

"Of course you did."

"It looks great. Really like the two of you having a tête-à-tête," Odele added, warming to her subject and ignoring the sarcasm.

"Did it also look as if I was going to kick him in the shins?"

"And I've already set up a print interview for the two of you with a trusted reporter," Odele went on as if she hadn't heard.

"I'm not looking for a protector. And have you even done a background check on Rick Serenghetti? Maybe he's the one I need safeguarding from!"

Rick was dangerous to her tranquility, but she didn't care to delve into the reasons why. He had a way of looking at her with a lazy, sultry gleam that she found…annoying—yes, definitely annoying.

She'd done a quick search online for him—*only* for the purpose of satisfying herself that he didn't have a criminal record, she told herself—and had come up with nothing. She supposed no news was good news.

"Who said anything about a bodyguard?" Odele said innocently. "This is to help everyone believe you two are an item."

So Rick had backed off the part about offering personal protection? Somehow she had her doubts. "He doesn't need to move in to do that. What ever happened to dating? We're going from zero to sixty."

"It's Hollywood. Pregnancies last five months, and babies arrive right after the wedding. Everything is fast here."

Chiara couldn't argue. Celebrities were well-known for trying to hide their pregnancies from the press until the second trimester or beyond.

"Do I need to resend you the latest headline about Michael Feran?" Odele asked.

"I've already read it. I should have taken a different surname when I started my career."

"Too late now, sweetie. Besides, the media would have found him anyway, and he'd still be giving you trouble."

"Yes, but it would have made the connection between us seem less close."

"Well, time to distance yourself by cozying up to a hot stuntman."

"I know I'm going to regret this," Chiara muttered.

"I'll arrange for him to move in at the end of the week," Odele responded brightly.

"The guest bedroom, Odele!"

Four

Rick roared up on his motorcycle.

Since he was in temporary digs, and most of his stuff was in storage, he didn't have much to bring to Chiara's house in the affluent Brentwood neighborhood. Instead, he'd had a taxi deposit his suitcases and duffel bags at the foot of Chiara's front steps shortly before his arrival midafternoon.

Looking up, he eyed the house. It was a modest size by Tinseltown standards. Three bedrooms and three baths, according to the write-up on a celebrity gossip site. Reminiscent of an English cottage, it had white stucco walls, an arched doorway and a pitched roof with cross-gables and a prominent chimney. Lush gardening added to the atmosphere of a place that might be featured in *Architectural Digest*.

He'd taken Odele's advice and planned to say nothing about being a bodyguard. As far as Chiara was concerned, he was here only as a pretend live-in boyfriend. He had no idea, however, how Odele had convinced Chiara to let him move in.

By the time he'd taken off his helmet, Chiara was standing on the front steps.

"Of course you'd ride a motorcycle," she commented.

He gave an insouciant smile.

"I thought it was an earthquake."

"I rock your world, huh?"

"Please."

He looked at her house. "Nice digs. I should have guessed a typical English-style cottage for you, Snow. But where's the thatched roof?"

"Wrong century," she responded. "Where do you call home?"

He gave a lopsided grin. "Technically a small apartment in West Hollywood, but my heart is always where there's a beautiful woman."

"I thought so."

He couldn't tell what she meant by her response. Still, he couldn't resist provoking her further. "Shouldn't we kiss for the benefit of the paparazzi and their long-range lenses?"

"There are no photographers," she scoffed.

"How do you know? One could be hiding in the bushes."

She eyed his suitcases. "I'll put you in the guest bedroom."

"Relegated to the couch already," he joked. "Are you going to do a media interview about our first lovers' spat?"

The temperature between them rose ten degrees, and even the planted geraniums perked up—they apparently liked a good show as much as anybody.

"Hilarious," Chiara shot back, "but it's a perfectly fine bed, not a couch."

"And you won't be in it."

She cast him a sweeping look. "Use your imagination. A make-believe relationship means pretend sex. But something tells me you have no problem with letting your dreams run wild."

"Will you still awaken me with a kiss, Snow White?"

She huffed. "You're hopeless. I don't do fairy tales, modern or otherwise."

"That's obvious."

"Don't act as if you're disappointed. Your forte is action flicks, not romantic comedies."

"Then why do I feel as if I'm trapped in a romance?" he murmured.

"Go blow something up and make yourself feel better."

"It's not that type of itch that I need to scratch."

She huffed and then turned toward her front door. "I'll have you checked for fleas then."

Rick stifled a grin. This was going to be one interesting stay.

After he got settled in the guest bedroom, he found Chiara in the large country-style kitchen. Warm beige

cabinets and butcher-block countertops added to the
warm atmosphere. Sniffing the air, he said, "Something smells delicious."

She glanced up from a saucepan on the range, edible enough herself to be a food advertiser's dream.
"Surprised?"

"That you cook? Gratified."

"Dinner is beef Stroganoff."

"Now I'm surprised. You're an actress who eats."

"Portion control is everything."

"Can cook. I'll check that little detail off my list."

She cast him a sidelong look, her cloud of dark
hair falling in tantalizing waves over one shoulder.
"What list?"

"The one that Odele gave me. A little quiz for the
both of us...so we can get acquainted. Be believable
as a couple."

Chiara frowned, and then muttered, "Odele leaves
nothing to chance. Next thing, she'll have us convincing the immigration service that we're not in a sham
marriage for a residency card."

"Because you need one...being from the Land of
Fairy Tales?" He almost got a smile out of her with
that.

"What do you—I mean, Odele—want to know?"

Rick consulted his cell phone. "What first attracted
you to me?"

Chiara spluttered and then set down her stirring
spoon with a *clack*. "This is never going to work."

"Come on, there must be something that you can
tell the reporters."

She looked flustered. "Does she ask you the same question about me?"

He lowered his eyelids. "What do you think?"

As the question hung there, Rick's mind skipped back to their stunts...the rehearsals...every single moment, in fact, that he'd become aware of her close by. The air had vibrated with sexual energy.

Chiara wet her lips. "I'll take that as a 'Yes, she did ask.'"

Rick gave her a seductive smile. "When you showed up for the rehearsal of our first stunt, I knew I was in trouble. You were beautiful and smart and had guts." He shrugged. "My fantasy woman. The perfect match."

Chiara blinked.

After a pause, he asked, "Sound good enough for an interview answer?"

She seemed to give herself a mental shake, and then pursed her lips. "Perfect."

He focused on her mouth. *Kissable, definitely.* "Great."

She slapped the lid on the saucepan and made for the kitchen door. "Things are simmering. Dinner will be ready in thirty minutes."

"It'll give you time to think of your own answer to Odele's question," he called after her, and could swear she muttered something under her breath.

But when she was gone, Rick acknowledged that much as he enjoyed teasing Chiara, the joke was on him. Because she was his dream woman. If only she wasn't also a publicity-hungry actress...

Through dinner, he and Chiara trod lightly around each other. The beef Stroganoff was delicious, and he helped clean up—a little surprised she didn't keep a full-time housekeeper even if she traveled a lot. Afterward, she excused herself and retreated to her room, announcing that she had to memorize her lines.

Left to his own devices, he took a quick tour of the house and grounds, familiarizing himself with its security…and possible vulnerability to intruders. Then, with nothing more to do, he headed to bed.

Passing Chiara's door, he could see a light beneath, and shook off thoughts of what she wore to bed and how her hair would look around her bare shoulders above a counterpane… Still, in the guest bedroom, he found himself punching his pillow multiple times before he drifted off to sleep.

"Rick?"

He opened his eyes and saw Chiara's shadowy silhouette in his bedroom doorway. His lips curved. Apparently she'd had a hard time sleeping, too.

She walked toward him, and he made no attempt to disguise his arousal—he'd been thinking about her. Her short slip with spaghetti straps hid little, her nipples jutting against the fabric. She had a fantastic figure. High breasts and an indented waist…softly curved hips. His fingers itched to touch her.

Instead, he propped himself on the pillows behind him.

She sat down on the side of the bed, and her hand brushed his erection.

He saw no prickliness—just need...for him.

"What can I do for you?" His voice came out as a rasp.

Chiara's eyes glowed in the dim light afforded by the moon. "I think you know."

She leaned closer. Her lips brushed his and her pretty breasts tantalized his bare chest.

He cupped the back of her head and brought her closer so he could deepen the kiss. His tongue swept inside her mouth, tangling and dueling with hers.

She moaned and sank against him, breaking the kiss just long enough to say, "Love me."

He needed no further invitation. He pulled her down onto the mattress next to him and covered her body with his.

She responded with the lack of inhibition that he'd hoped for, arching toward him and opening in invitation, her arms encircling his neck as she met the ardor of his kiss.

His only thought was to get even closer...to sink into her welcoming warmth and find oblivion.

It would be sweet release from the restless need that had been consuming him...

Rick awoke with a start. He couldn't tell what had jerked him from his fantasy, but the room was empty, and he was alone in his bed.

He was also frustrated and aroused.

He groaned. *Yup.* It was going to be torture acting as if he were Chiara's boyfriend and hiding the fact that he was her protector.

* * *

The next morning, Chiara was up early for the drive to Novatus Studio. She donned jeans and a knit top. No use prettying up since she'd be sitting in a makeup chair at work soon enough. In fact, it was so early, she figured she might be able to get in a few minutes to study today's lines of dialogue before the drive to the lot.

Concentrate, that's what she had to do. But she hadn't slept well. In bed last night, she'd stared up at the ceiling, very aware of Rick's presence in her house.

What attracted her to him?

He was the epitome of rough manliness—cool, tough and exuding sex appeal. His green eyes were fascinatingly multihued, and even the hard, sculpted plains of his face invited detailed study by touch and, yes, taste.

A woman could feel safe and sheltered in his arms.

And there was the problem. She'd learned a long time ago not to rely on any man. Starting with her father, who'd disappeared from her life at a young age, and had become a gambling addict and reprobate.

She didn't hear a sound from Rick's room, so she tiptoed downstairs with script in hand.

When she reached the kitchen, she was taken aback to spot him sitting outside on the veranda, gazing at the sunrise, dressed in black denim jeans and a maroon tee. He looked peaceful and relaxed, so far from the constant motion and barely leashed energy that she was used to from him.

As if sensing her presence, he turned and met her gaze. Rising, he gave a jaunty salute with the mug in his hand and said, "Good morning."

"I didn't hear you," she blurted as he entered through the French doors.

"We stuntmen can be stealthy."

She lowered her lashes and swept him with a surreptitious look. His jeans hugged lean hips and outlined muscular legs. The tee covered a flat chest and biceps that were defined but not brawny. He had the physique and face for a movie screen, except there was nothing manicured about him. Rick had a rough male aura instead of polish.

She looked at the cup in his hands. "I didn't even smell the brew."

"It's not coffee. It's a vitamin power drink."

Ugh. "For your superhero strength."

"Of course." He gave her a wicked smile. "Helps with the stamina. Sleep well?"

"For sure. And you?" She refused to give an inch, treating him with cool civility, even if that smile made her body tighten.

"Naturally."

The truth was she'd lain awake and tossed around for close to two hours. She wondered how she was going to maintain this charade...especially since Rick was adept at provoking her. And she refused...*refused*...to dwell on his kiss.

"Nice story about your father in the news. I had time to catch up on the headlines while I waited for you to come down, Sleeping Beauty."

Damn it. She should have gotten up even earlier. "My father?"

"Yeah, you know, the guy who shares a last name with you."

"That's all we have in common," she muttered.

"Nice story about the card counting recently."

"Maybe he'll stay out of trouble now that he's been barred from his favorite haunts." Casinos were Michael Feran's drug of choice.

"Is that what you're hoping?"

"Why are we discussing this?"

He shrugged. "I figured we should talk about the reason we're together." A smile teased his lips. "It seems logical."

So he wanted an extension of yesterday's get-to-know-you? *No, thanks.* Not that last night's question had haunted her sleep or anything. "We're not together."

"It's what the tabloids think that matters."

Argh.

"So Michael Feran is a sensitive topic."

Chiara walked to the kitchen cabinets. "Only in as much as he's a liar, gambler and cheat."

"Hmm…must be hard to share the same surname."

She got a glass and poured herself some water from the fridge's water filter.

"Eight glasses a day?"

She glanced at him. "What do you think? It's good for the complexion."

"You're very disciplined."

She took a sip. "I have to be."

"Because your father isn't?"

"I don't define myself relative to him."

Rick's lips twitched. "Okay, so you're not your father."

"Of course."

"How old were you when he walked out?"

She put down the glass. "Nearly five. But even when he was there, he wasn't really. He disappeared for stretches. Some of it was spent touring as a sax player with a band. Then he moved out for good a few days before my fifth birthday."

"Must have been rough."

"Not really. The party went on without him." She remembered the pink heart piñata. Her first major role was putting on a smile for the photos when it was just her and her mother.

"Did he ever try coming back?"

"There were a few flyovers until I became a teenager."

"Brief?"

"Very." Either her parents would argue, or Michael Feran would quickly move on to his next big thing.

"Right." Rick looked as if he'd drawn his own conclusions.

"Why are we talking about this?" she asked again, her voice sharp.

"I need to get the story straight so I'm not contradicting you when I speak."

"Well, there's nothing to tell."

"That's not what the press thinks."

Yup, he had her there. Which was the crux of her

problem. Straightening her shoulders, she grabbed her car keys from the kitchen counter. On second thought, she could have breakfast at the studio—there was always food around. "Well, I'm off. See you on set."

"I'm coming with you," Rick responded casually. "Or rather, you're coming with me."

She stopped and faced him. "Excuse me?"

"My car or yours?"

"Do you have an endless supply of pickup lines?"

"Do you want to find out?"

"No!"

"That's what I thought you'd say." He took a sip from his mug. "How can we be two lovebirds if we don't arrive together?"

"We're trying to be discreet at work."

"But not for the press."

"Anyway, you own a motorcycle."

"Look outside. I had my car deposited here early this morning by a concierge service."

Rats. He'd been up even earlier than she'd thought. She tossed him a suspicious look and then walked over to peer out the French doors. She spotted a Range Rover in the drive. "Lovely."

"I think so."

She glanced back at Rick with suspicion, but he just returned a bland look. Another of his sexual innuendoes? Because it was impossible to tell what he'd been referring to—her or the car.

Then she sighed. She had to pick her battles, and it was clear the drive to the office was not one worth fighting over.

Rick walked toward her, pausing to glance at a script that she'd left on the counter yesterday. "It's early. Want me to quiz you on your lines?"

"No!" Not least because there was a scene were the leads got flirty.

Rick raised an eyebrow and then shrugged. "Suit yourself but the offer stands. Anytime."

Yup, he was an anytime, anywhere kind of guy.

"What else are we supposed to do while we're shacked up together?" he asked, his eyes laughing at her.

She raised an eyebrow. "Go to work?"

Within the hour, she and Rick pulled up to the gate to Novatus Studio in his car.

Rick rolled down his window in order to give his identification to security, and with a sixth sense, Chiara turned her head and spotted a hovering figure nearby. The flash of a paparazzi camera was familiar.

"Odele," she muttered, facing forward again.

There was a good chance that her manager had tipped off a photographer so someone could snap her and Rick arriving *together* at the studio. Odele was determined to give this story her personal spin.

Rick gave an amused look. "She thinks of everything."

Rick tried to be on his best behavior, but having some fun was oh-so-tempting…

The Living Room on the first floor of The Peninsula Beverly Hills was nothing if not a den for power brokers, so he supposed it was perfect for a print interview over afternoon tea with *WE Magazine*—which wanted the dishy scoop on Chiara's new relationship.

Rick eyed the sumptuous repast set out on the coffee table before them: finger sandwiches, scones and an assortment of petite pastries. Arranged by Odele, of course, the afternoon tea in The Living Room was worthy of a queen. Of course, all of it went untouched.

This wasn't about food, but business. *Showtime in Hollywood.*

When he and Chiara had arrived at Novatus Studio that morning, Odele had surprised them with the news that she'd arranged a friendly press interview for them later the same day. Chiara was already scheduled to have the cover of the next issue of *WE Magazine* in order to promote the upcoming release of *Pegasus Pride*, but Odele had deftly arranged for it to become a joint interview about her new relationship. He and Chiara had left work early, because Odele had already spoken to Dan, the director, about their appointment. Dan had been happy to oblige if it meant more positive ink ahead of the release of the film—everyone was banking on it opening big at the box office.

Rick had to hand it to Chiara's manager—she wasted no time. But he knew what Odele was thinking—better to get ahead of the gossip by getting your own version of the story out there before anyone else's. So he'd gone along with the whole deal.

Too bad Chiara herself didn't want him here. But Odele had insisted, arguing his presence would make the relationship more believable. As Odele had put it, *Readers inhale romance. Touch each other a lot.* To which Chiara had responded, *Odele, I'm not making out in public for the benefit of gawkers.*

Now, at his sudden grin at the recollection, Chiara shot him a repressive look. She'd already told him she saw his role here as a yes-man supporting player. He figured he could bridge the gap between stuntman and Prince Charming easily enough, but if Chiara thought he'd toady to a gossip columnist, she had another think coming. He stretched and then settled one arm on the back of the sofa—because he knew it would drive Chiara crazy.

The couch was in a cozy and semiprivate corner. The interviewer, Melody Banyon—who looked to be in her late forties and was a dead ringer for Mindy Kaling—leaned forward in her armchair. "So was it love at first sight?"

From the corner of his eye, Rick noticed Chiara's elbow inching toward him, ready to jab in case he made a flippant comment. But then Chiara just smiled at him before purring, "Well, I don't usually notice the stuntmen on my movie sets…"

Rick glanced at the interviewer and a corner of his mouth lifted. "You could say Chiara's manager played matchmaker. She thought we'd be perfect for each other."

Chiara's eyes widened, but then she tossed him a grateful look. "Yes, Odele is always looking out for my best interests…"

Melody gave a satisfied smile. "Great, just great."

Repositioning the voice recorder on the table before them, she looked back and forth between her interview subjects. "And I understand you two just moved in together?"

"Yup," Rick spoke up, unable to resist. "Like yesterday." It was also roughly when their whole "relationship" had started.

Chiara shot him a quelling look, and he tossed back an innocent one. He moved his arm off the sofa, gave her shoulder a squeeze, and then leaned in and nuzzled her temple for a quick kiss.

"Mmm," Melody said, as if tasting a delicious story, "you two move fast."

Rick relaxed against the sofa again, and responded sardonically, "You don't know the half of it."

He knew he risked Chiara's wrath, and he was surprised to find himself relishing the challenge of sparring with her again. No doubt about it—they set sparks off in each other. And it would probably carry over to the bedroom.

He glanced at Chiara's profile. She was a beautiful woman. Winged brows, pink bow lips, thick, rich chocolate hair and a figure that was hourglass without being voluptuous. She was also talented and tough enough to play a kick-ass action movie heroine and do her own stunts. He had to respect that—all the while being attracted as hell—even though he knew celebrity actresses like her couldn't be trusted.

They were duplicitous—they had to be for the press. *Like right now.*

Chiara seemed chummy with Melody—as if they

were friends, or at least acquaintances from way back. Melody asked a few questions about *Pegasus Pride*, and Chiara answered, while Rick threw in a few sentences at the end.

He wasn't the star attraction here, and there was no use pretending otherwise. Sure, he had a lot riding on this film—money and otherwise—but he wouldn't be why this movie succeeded, or not, at the box office. Chiara was the public face of *Pegasus Pride*.

After a few minutes, Melody changed the subject, mentioning the upcoming Ring of Hope Gala to Benefit Children's Charities, for which half of Hollywood turned out. "So give me the scoop, Chiara." Her voice dipped conspiratorially. "What will you be wearing?"

"I haven't decided yet. There are two dresses…"

"Give me the details on both!" Melody said, her face avid with anticipation.

Rick suppressed a grunt. As far as he was concerned, a dress was a dress. He didn't care what it was made out of—whether a pride of lions had to be sacrificed for the embellishment, or the designer used recycled garbage bags. His youngest sibling might be an up-and-comer in the fashion business, but it was all the same to Rick—or as his sister liked to say, *Bless your style-deaf soul.*

"There's a one-shoulder pale blue column dress from Elie Saab. The other gown is a red chiffon—"

"Oh, I love both! Don't you, Rick?"

If it wasn't for Chiara's significant look, Rick would have answered that *naked* was his first preference. Chiara had a body that invited fantasies even, or especially, if she was aiming verbal barbs at him.

He settled back. "I don't know…isn't pale blue the color for Cinderella?"

Chiara turned to him and smiled, even as her eyes shot a warning. "Wrong fairy tale."

When Melody just appeared confused, Chiara cleared her throat. "Well, keep your eyes open on the night of the gala to find out which dress I go with."

The reporter pressed Stop on her recorder. "So when am I going to see you again, Chiara? Girls' night sometime at Marmont? Paparazzi snapped Leo there just last week."

Rick raised his eyebrows. From the lack of a ring, Rick deduced Melody was divorced, widowed or had never married. "You ladies do go for the chills and thrills."

Chateau Marmont was a trendy celebrity haunt. Some booked one of the hotel rooms for privacy, and others just went to party and be seen. But he preferred his thrills a little more real than a Leonardo DiCaprio sighting.

"I'd love to, Melody," Chiara said, "but can I take a rain check? This movie is wearing me out—" she looked down demurely "—when Rick isn't."

Yup, strong acting chops.

Melody laughed. "Of course. I understand."

When Melody excused herself a moment later in order to freshen up, Rick regarded the woman who'd been driving him crazy. "So… I wear you out?"

Chiara flushed. "Don't look at me that way."

"Mmm. The image of us and a bed is sort of stuck in my mind."

Chiara shifted, and her skirt rode up her leg.

He focused on her calves. She had spectacular legs. He'd seen them encased in skintight denim on set, and in a barely there miniskirt in a photo that had circulated online. He imagined those legs wrapped around him as he lost himself inside her...

On a whim, he reached out and took her hand, and caressed the back of it with his thumb.

"What are you doing?"

Was it his imagination or did her voice sound a little uneven?

"Move closer," he murmured. "There's a photographer watching us from across the room."

Her eyes held his. "What? Where?"

"Don't look." Then he leaned in, his gaze lowering.

Chiara parted her lips on an indrawn breath.

Rick touched his mouth to hers.

When Chiara made a sound at the back of her throat, he deepened the kiss. He stroked and teased, wanting more from her, craving more and not caring where they were. When she opened for him, he fanned the flames of their passion, cupping her face with his hand as she leaned closer.

When her breast brushed his arm, he tensed and stopped himself from bringing his hand up to cup the soft mound in public. He wanted to crash through her barriers, making his head spin with the speed of it.

As if sensing someone approaching, Chiara pulled back and muttered, "We have to stop."

Rick spotted Melody walking back from across the room, a big grin on her face. Obviously the reporter had seen the kiss. Odele would be pleased. "Not if we're going to pretend to be a couple."

When the reporter drew near, she teased, "Did I say you two are fast? Now, that moment would have provided some photo op for the magazine!"

Rick settled back and forced a grin for the reporter's benefit. "We'd be happy to give a repeat performance."

"No, we wouldn't," Chiara interjected, but then she smiled for Melody's benefit. "I'll make sure you get plenty of good pictures for the cover story at the photo shoot tomorrow."

"Of course," Melody said politely, maintaining her perkiness as she sat down to gather her things.

Rick hadn't gotten an invitation to the photo shoot—which was just as well. They were boring and went on for hours. Apparently, though, even Odele had drawn the line at a cozy tableau of him and Chiara with their arms around each other.

"Do you have a cover line yet for this article, Melody?" Chiara asked, her face suddenly turning droll. "Or has Odele already suggested one?"

Rick knew from his experience with movie promotions that the cover line was the front cover text that accompanied a magazine article: *From Tears to Triumph*, *I'm Lucky to Be Alive*, or even the vague but trustworthy standby, *My Turn to Talk*.

"No," Melody said, "Odele hasn't offered anything."

"How about 'Chiara Feran—True Love at Last'?" he offered drily.

Melody brightened. "I love it. What about you, Chiara?"

Chiara looked as if she was ready to kick him out of this interview, and Rick suppressed a laugh.

Oh, yeah, this was going to be a roller coaster of a relationship. *Make-believe* relationship.

Five

Soon after she and Rick arrived at her house—a place that she used to consider her haven and sanctuary until Rick moved in—she decided to escape to the exercise room to let off steam. Every once in a while, the urge to do the right thing and work out for the sake of her career kicked in, so she changed into a sports bra and stretchy pedal pusher exercise pants.

It had been a long day, and she'd risen early only to find Rick in her kitchen. At the studio, she'd gotten prepped in her makeup chair and then shot a few scenes. Afterward, she'd still had to be *on*, public persona in place, for the interview with Melody. It hadn't helped that the whole time she'd been aware of Rick lounging beside her—his big, hard body making the sofa seem tiny and crowded.

He'd enjoyed toying with her, too, during the interview. She'd been on pins and needles the whole time, wondering whether he'd say the wrong thing and Melody would see through their charade.

Except the kiss at the end had been all too real. She'd tasted his need and his slow-burn desire underneath the playfulness, and she'd responded to it.

I have to be more careful.

And on that thought, she entered the exercise room and came to a dead halt.

Apparently Rick had had the same idea about burning off steam. And in a sleeveless cutoff tee, it was clear he was in phenomenal shape.

She'd seen her share of beautiful people in Hollywood. But Rick was…impressive. He had washboard abs, a sprinkling of hair on his chest and muscles so defined they looked as if they could have been sculpted by a Renaissance master.

She shouldn't be once-overing him. She was still annoyed with his behavior in front of Melody that afternoon.

Rick looked up and gave her a careless lopsided smile. "Enjoying the view?"

A wave of embarrassment heated her face. "Nothing I haven't seen before."

"Yeah, but I'm not airbrushed."

And there was the problem in a nutshell.

"Need an exercise buddy?"

Oh, no. They were so not going to do this together. "I don't need you to act as my workout instructor. I've been doing fine on my own."

"Yeah," he drawled, "I can tell."

She gave him a quelling look and walked toward the weight bench.

He followed her and then scanned the weights. He lifted one of the lighter ones as if it were a feather and placed it on the bar.

She put her hands on her hips. "What do you think you're doing?"

"Helping you out, but not as much as I'd like."

"You're already doing more than I want, so let's call it a draw and say we're splitting the difference."

He quirked his lips. "Just trying to get you to release that pent-up energy and frustration."

She narrowed her eyes and then lay back on the bench as he fixed the weight on the other side. Unfortunately she hadn't anticipated how much he seemed to be looming over her from this angle.

She flexed and then grasped the barbell. Before she could do more, however, Rick adjusted her grip.

"I started with sixty pounds," he said, stepping back. "That's about right for a woman your size."

Chiara wondered how much he lifted. He'd hoisted her with amazing agility and ease during their stunts...

Then she turned her attention back to the weights, took a breath and began lifting. Once, twice... Rick faded into the background as she brought the same attention to the task as she did to acting.

"Slow and smooth," he said after a few minutes. "Slow and smooth... That's right."

Damn it. Chiara's rhythm hitched as she brought

the weight back up again and then down. She refused to look at Rick. He was either a master at sexual innuendo or set on unintentionally making her lose her mind.

She gritted her teeth and lifted the weight a few more times. After what seemed like an eternity, during which she refused to show any weakness, Rick caught the barbell and placed it on the nearby rack.

Chiara concentrated on slowing her breathing, but her chest still rose and fell from the exertion.

Rick leaned over her, bracing himself with one hand on the metal leg of the weight bench. "Nice work."

They weren't touching but he was a hair's breadth away—so close that she could get lost in the gold-shot green of his eyes. Her mind wandered back to their last kiss…

He quirked his lips as if he knew what she was thinking. "Want to indulge again?"

She pretended not to understand his meaning. "No, thanks. I'm dieting. You know Hollywood actresses. We're always trying to shed a few pounds."

Rick's eyes crinkled. "Seems more like fasting to me."

Damn him. As a celebrity, it wasn't as if she could just get online, or even on an app, and hook up with someone. There was her public image to consider, as Odele never stopped reminding her, and she didn't want to be exploited for someone else's gain. As a result, she'd had far fewer romantic partners than the press liked to imagine. These days, a lot of men were intimidated by her status. But not Rick. He was just a lone stuntman, but he had enough ego for an entire football team.

Still, need hummed within her, and her skin shivered with awareness. What was it with this man? He had a talent for getting under her defenses, and together they were combustible.

"Have I been doing it right?" His eyes laughed at her.

"What?"

"The kissing."

If the response he stirred in her was any indication, then…yeah. She tingled right now—wanting him closer against her better judgment. "All wrong."

"Then we need to practice." His lips curved in a sultry smile. "For the photographers and their cameras."

She'd walked into that one. "There isn't one here right now."

"Then we'll need to make this real instead of make-believe," he muttered as he focused on her mouth. "You have the fullest, most kissable lips."

Chiara inhaled a quick little breath. It was heady being the focus of Rick's attention. He brought the same intensity to kissing as he did to his stunts.

But instead of immediately touching his mouth to hers this time, he surprised her by smoothing a hand down her side.

She shivered, and her nipples puckered, pushing against her sports bra. She itched to explore him the way he was doing to her. She raised her hand to push him away, but instead it settled on his chest, where she felt the strong, steady beat of his heart.

"That's right," he encouraged. "Touch me. Make me feel."

She parted her lips, and this time he did settle his mouth on hers. She felt a little zing, and was surrounded by his unique male scent.

His chest pressed down on the pillow of her breasts, but he didn't give her all his weight, which was still braced on his arms.

Wrapped in his intoxicating closeness, she felt him everywhere, even on the parts of her body that weren't touching his.

His hand cupped her between her thighs, where her tight spandex shorts were the only barrier between her heat and his. He stroked her with his thumb, again and again, until she tore her mouth from his and gasped with need.

She grasped his wrist, but it was too late. Her body splintered, spasming with completion and yet unfulfilled desire.

When she looked up, she was caught by his glittering gaze. She was vulnerable and exposed, more so even than when they'd been hanging from a helicopter and his embrace had been a haven.

She could tell he wanted her, but he was holding himself in check, his breathing heavy.

Sanity slowly returned. This was so wrong.

"Let me up," she said huskily.

He straightened, and then tugged on her hand to help her up.

"I don't want this," she said, standing and knowing the last thing she needed was to feel this way—especially when wrong felt...right.

"Sometimes what we think we should want is beside the point."

She wanted to argue, but for once, she didn't know what to say.

"I'm going to take a cold shower," he said with a rueful smile, and then turned.

She half expected a teasing addition—*Want to join me?*

But he said nothing further, and somehow she found his seriousness more troubling than his playfulness.

Bed & Breakfast in Brentwood. Chiara Feran and Her Stuntman Seen Moving in Together.

Chiara stalked back to her trailer along a dirt path, her scene complete. Filming had moved for today from the Novatus Studio lot to nearby Griffith Park.

The blog *Celebrity Dish* had scooped *WE Magazine* and run a relationship story about her and Rick. Melody should still be happy about her exclusive interview, but it hadn't taken long for the gossip to start making the rounds...

Chiara attributed her bad mood to lack of coffee... and a certain stuntman.

Yesterday afternoon, they'd had a near tryst on her weight bench. There was no telling what he was capable of if he stayed in her house much longer.

She'd shown up at work at six in the morning intent

on avoiding Rick, and had sat in the makeup chair. It was now ten, and there was still no sign of him. After their encounter in the exercise room, she'd heard him shower and leave her house. He still hadn't returned when she'd gone to bed hours later.

Perhaps he'd met and hooked up with a woman. Not that it was her business. Even if it meant he'd gone straight from her arms to those of another … *Damn it.*

At least *Pegasus Pride* would wrap soon. They were in the last days of filming. The scenes that she'd been in with Rick acting as a body double for her co-star Adrian had been thankfully few.

Head down, she turned a corner…and collided with a solid male chest.

The air rushed out of her, and then she gasped.

But before she could wonder whether her favorite fan had made a surprise appearance again, strong arms steadied her, and she looked up into Rick's green eyes.

"You."

"For two people who are roommates, we hardly ever run into each other," he said in an ironic tone.

Chiara blinked. His hands were still cupping her upper arms, the wall of his chest a mere hair's breadth away. The heat emanated from him like a palpable thing.

"It's a big house and an even larger movie location." She sounded breathless and chalked it up to having the air nearly knocked out of her.

He was irritating but also impossible to ignore—

and she'd been throwing her best acting skills at the problem.

"Miss me?" he teased drily. "I thought we were supposed to be joined at the hip these days."

How could she answer that one? After he'd left last night, she'd succumbed to a restless night's sleep. He'd left her satisfied and bereft at the same time. Sure, she'd gotten release, but they'd missed out on the ultimate joining, and hours later, her body had craved it. At least he wasn't openly chastising her for her artful dodge that morning.

He stepped closer and eased her chin up, his gaze focused on her lips. "I missed you."

"The mouth that can't stop telling you off?"

He gave her a crooked smile. "We'd be good in bed. There's too much combustible energy between us. Admit it."

"Can't you tell good acting when you see it?"

"That was no act. If that wasn't an orgasm last night, I'll stand naked under the Hollywood sign over there." With a nod of his head, he indicated the iconic landmark in the distance.

"We are acting. This is fake. We're on a movie set!"

"Yup," he drawled and glanced around, "and I don't see any cameras rolling right now. Just because we're playing to the media doesn't mean we can't have fun along the way."

She didn't do *fun*. She left that to her dice-rolling father, who'd run away from responsibility—a wife, a child, a home...

"Oh, I like it!"

Chiara turned and spotted Odele.

"Did I interrupt something? Or let me rephrase that one—I hope I was interrupting something!"

"He needs to go," Chiara retorted.

Odele looked from her to Rick and back. "What went wrong? It's only been—" she checked her watch "—two days."

"A lover's spat," Rick joked. "We can't keep our hands off each other."

Odele's eyes gleamed behind her red glasses. "You can't quit now. The press is reporting Chiara's father was tossed out of a Vegas casino."

Rick quirked a brow at Chiara.

"On top of it," Odele went on, "there's a big fundraiser tomorrow night, and I managed to secure a ticket for Chiara's date."

"And let's not forget *WE* just got the exclusive interview that *we* are an item," Rick continued drolly.

Chiara faced her nemesis. "You are impossible."

"Just acting the part."

"You're giving an Oscar-worthy performance in a B movie."

"I believe in doing my best," Rick intoned solemnly. "My mother raised me right."

She wanted to claim his *best* wasn't good enough, but the truth was he'd been…impressive so far. "This isn't working."

"You don't want me?" He adopted a wounded expression, but his eyes laughed at her.

Grr. "I'm stuck with you!"

"Then why don't you make the most of it?" His voice was smooth as massage lotion. "Who knows? We might even have fun together."

The last thing she needed was his hands on her again. "*Fun* is not the word that comes to mind. This is crazy. Are we nuts?"

"You know the answer to that question. I hang from helicopters for a living—"

"Clearly the altitude has addled your mind."

"—and you are an actress and celebrity."

"*Fame* is a dirty word in your book?"

Rick shrugged. "I'm camera-shy. Call it middle-child syndrome. I leave the high-profile celebrity stuff to my older and younger brothers."

She frowned. "You're an agoraphobic stuntman?"

He bit back a laugh. "Not quite, but putting on the glitz isn't my thing."

"Odele just mentioned we have a big fund-raiser to attend tomorrow night," she countered. "And since you signed up for the boyfriend gig, you'll need to put on a tux."

"Trust me, you'll like me better naked."

Chiara felt her cheeks heat, and on top of that, her manager was tracking everything like a talent agent on the scent of a movie deal.

She narrowed her eyes at Rick. "Oh? Is that the usual attire for reclusive stuntmen?"

He gave a lazy smile. "If we live together much longer, you'll find out."

She hated his casual self-assurance. And what was worse, he was probably right…

Chiara gave her manager a what-have-you-gotten-me-into look, but Odele returned it with a beatific one of her own.

"I came to tell you that you're needed. Dan wants to reshoot a scene," Odele said.

Chiara wasn't normally enthusiastic about retakes, but right now she thought of it as a lucky break...

Hours later, during some downtime in his schedule, Rick sat in a chair outside the gym trailer, his legs propped on a nearby bench. He consulted his cell phone to make sure he was caught up on work.

Often his emails were mundane matters sent by a business partner, but today, lucky him, he had something more salacious to chew over. All courtesy of *Celebrity Dish*—and a specific actress who'd occupied way more of his thoughts than he cared to admit.

After his encounter with Chiara in her exercise room yesterday afternoon, he'd done the only thing that he could do in the face of frustration and lack of consummation: he'd taken a cold shower and then sat alone at a nearby sports bar to have dinner.

Still, now that the story had progressed in the media to him and Chiara shacking up, Rick knew he'd better tackle his family. In the next moment, his cell phone buzzed, and Rick noted it was Jordan before answering the call.

"Wow, you move fast," his brother said without preamble. "One day you're denying there's anything going on, the next you're moving in together."

"Hilarious."

"Mom asked. Has she rung you yet?"

"Nope." Camilla Serenghetti was probably vac-illating between worry and being ecstatic that her middle son might have gotten into a serious relation-ship—preferably one heading toward marriage and children.

"She's concerned some temptress has worked her wiles on you, and not just on the big screen, either. I told her that you're not innocent and naive enough to resist a beautiful woman."

"Finger-pointing never got you anywhere, Jordan."

"Except for some scratches and bruises from you and Cole in retribution. But don't worry, I bounced back."

"Clearly," Rick responded drily.

"Mom is talking about coming to the West Coast to tape an episode of her cooking show. You know, do something different and expand the audience, and if I'm not mistaken—" his brother's voice dripped dry humor "—she wants to check up on you."

No, no and no. The last thing he needed was for his mother to add a sideshow to the ongoing drama with Chiara—though Camilla Serenghetti would no doubt easily become best buds with Odele. Two peas in a pod. Or as the Italians liked to say, *due gocce d'acqua*—like two drops of water. *In a pot of boil-ing pasta water.* Still, the thought gave him an idea…

"Mom can't come here."

"She's worried about the show. The station is under new management and she wants to make a good im-pression."

"Fine. I'll go to her."

The idea was brilliant. If he delivered Chiara Feran to his mother's show, he'd drive up ratings for a program that was only in local syndication. And it would add steam in the press to his and Chiara's supposed relationship. All while getting Chiara out of her house in LA and away from her crazy fan.

It was fantastic…clever…an idea worthy of Odele.

Rick suppressed a smile. Chiara's manager would love it.

"You're serious?" his brother asked.

"Yup." If he was going to engage in this charade, he was going to be all in.

With that in mind, he ended his call with Jordan and went looking for his favorite actress.

Things had slowed down on set because Adrian Collins didn't like some of his lines and had holed up in his trailer with a red pen. Rick would have gotten involved and gone to read the riot act to the male lead, but he didn't like to blow his cover. Not even Dan knew how much he had invested in this movie.

Besides, Adrian's antics were mild in comparison to other off-camera drama he'd witnessed on movie sets—stars kicking each other, hurling curses and insults, and throwing tantrums worthy of a two-year-old while breaking props. Yet another reason he hadn't gotten involved with mercurial actresses…until now.

As luck would have it, he soon caught up with Chiara some distance from the parked movie trailers. She was walking back alone, picking her way along a dusty path, apparently having finished filming another scene.

Maybe it was unfulfilled sexual desire, maybe it was the picture she presented, but his senses got overloaded seeing her again. Since this morning, she'd changed into business attire because her scenes called for her to have escaped from a federal office building. She was wearing a pencil skirt paired with sky-high black pumps and a white shirt open to show a bit a cleavage. The effect was sexy in an understated way.

He liked the way the light caught in her dark halo of hair—which was just the right length for him to run his fingers through in the throes of passion. His body tightened.

He wasn't one to be overcome by lust—particularly where actresses were concerned—but Chiara was just the package to press his buttons. He hadn't been kidding when he'd said she was his type. His brothers would say he was attracted to women who were a study in contrasts: dark hair against a palate of smooth skin; humor and passion; light and hidden depths… On top of it all, Chiara was blessed with a great figure, which was emphasized at the moment by a come-hither outfit made for the big screen…and male fantasies.

He, on the other hand, was in his usual stunt clothes for this movie: a ripped tee, makeup meant to resemble dirt smeared on his abs, an ammo belt across his chest and another one slug low on his hips with an unloaded gun. He felt…uncivilized.

And the setting was appropriate. They were at the

bottom of a canyon, surrounded by mountain roads and not far from actual caves. Only the presence of the Hollywood sign spoiled the effect of unspoiled nature.

Still, he tried for some semblance of polite conversation when they came abreast of each other. Thanks to Jordan, he had a brilliant idea—one that should deal with multiple problems at once. "I have a favor to ask."

She looked at him warily. "Which is?"

He cleared his throat. "I'd like you to appear on my mother's cooking show."

Her jaw went slack. "What?"

He shrugged. "If you appear on her show, it'll feed the rumors that we're involved. Isn't that what you want?"

"Your mother has a cooking show?"

He nodded. "It's on local TV in Boston and a few other markets, and it films not far from my hometown of Welsdale in western Massachusetts. *Flavors of Italy with Camilla Serenghetti.*"

Chiara's lips twitched. "So you're not the Serenghetti closest to fame? I'm shocked."

"Not by a long shot," he returned sardonically. "Not only is Mom ahead of me, but my brothers and sister are, too."

Chiara looked curious. "Really?"

He nodded. "You don't watch hockey."

"Should I?"

"My kid brother plays for the New England Razors, and my older brother used to."

She seemed as if she was trying to pull up a recollection.

"Jordan and Cole Serenghetti," he supplied.

"And your sister is…?"

"The youngest, but determined not to be left behind." He cracked a grin. "She's a big feminist."

"Naturally. With three older brothers, I imagine she had to be."

"She had a badass left kick in karate, but these days she's rechanneled the anger into a fashion design business."

Chiara's eyes widened. "Ooh, I like it already it."

So did he… Why hadn't he dreamed it up before? He had an opening with Chiara that he'd been too blind to see till now. "Mia would love it if you wore one of her creations."

"I thought I was helping your mother."

"Both." He toasted his brilliance. "You can wear Mia's designs on the cooking show."

Chiara threw up her hands. "You've thought of everything!"

Rick narrowed his eyes. "Not everything. I still need to figure out what to do about your overenthusiastic fan and your Vegas-loving father. Give me time."

Number three on his list was getting her into bed, but he wasn't going to mention that. He didn't examine his motives closely, except he was nursing one sad case of sexual frustration since their truncated tryst on her weight bench late yesterday. He tucked his fingers into his pockets to resist the urge to touch her…

He cleared his throat. "It would mean a lot to her

if you made an appearance as a guest. The show is doing well. The name recently changed from *Flavors of Italy* to *Flavors of Italy with Camilla Serenghetti*. But the station is under new management, and Mom wants to make a good impression."

"Of course," Chiara deadpanned. "It's a slow climb up the ladder of fame. I can relate."

"Mom's is more of a short stepladder."

"What happens when your mother and I land on the cover of *WE Magazine* together?" Chiara quipped. "Will you be able to deal with being caught between two famous women?"

"I'll cross that bridge when I come to it," Rick replied drolly. "And knowing Mom, she'll want to be on the magazine with the both of us, like a hovering fairy godmother."

"She sounds like a character."

"You don't know the half of it."

"This is serious," she remarked drily. "You're bringing me home to meet Mama."

"In a sense," he said noncommittally—because what he wanted to do was bring her home to bed. "She'd be even more impressed if you'd starred in an Italian telenovela."

"A soap opera?" Chiara responded. "Actually I was a guest on a couple of episodes of *Sotto Il Sole*."

Rick's eyebrows rose.

"It was before I became known in the States," she added. "My character wound up in a coma and was taken off life support."

"They didn't like your acting?"

"No, they just needed more melodrama. My character was an American so it didn't matter if I spoke Italian well."

"Still, my mother will eat it up." He flashed a grin. "No pun intended."

In fact, Rick suspected his mother would love everything about Chiara Feran. Their relationship "breakup," which inevitably loomed on the horizon, would disappoint his mother more than a recipe that didn't work out. He'd have to fake bodily injury and blame the rupture with Chiara on the distance created by their two careers...

"What about filming?" Chiara asked with a frown.

"We're in the last few days. Then Dan will move to editing. I can arrange with Odele for us to fly to Boston once you're done with your scenes. Mom's taping can wait till then." He didn't add he still had to broach the subject with his mother, but she'd no doubt be thrilled to move heaven and earth with her producers in order to fit a star of Chiara's caliber into the schedule.

"Where will we stay?" Chiara pressed.

Rick could tell she was debating her options, but the wavering was a good sign. He shrugged, deciding to seem nonchalant in order to soothe any doubts she had.

"I've got an apartment in Welsdale."

"Oh?"

"It has a guest bedroom." Still, he hoped to entice her into making their relationship in the bedroom more real—purely for the sake of their romantic believability in front of the press, of course.

"Naturally."

"Don't worry, though," he said, making his tone gently mocking. "There'll be enough luxuries for an A-list celeb."

Chiara narrowed her eyes. "You think I can't rough it?"

He let his silence speak for him.

"As a matter of fact, I was born and raised in Rhode Island. I'm used to New England winters."

"Of course, Miss Rhode Island should visit her old stomping grounds."

"I was an undergraduate at Brown."

"Rubbing shoulders with other celebrity kids?"

"Financial aid. Where did you get your stunt degree?"

He quirked his lips. "Boston College. It's a family tradition."

"Now you've surprised me. I expected the school of hard knocks... So, what have you told your family about us?"

He shrugged. "They read *WE Magazine*." He flashed a smile. "They know I have the goods."

Chiara rolled her eyes. "In other words, they think we really are an item?"

"My ego wouldn't have it any other way."

"I'm not surprised."

Rick heard a noise, and then felt a telltale little jolt, followed by a gentle rocking.

Chiara's eyes widened.

"Did you feel that?"

She nodded.

Earthquakes were common in Southern California, but only a few were strong enough to be felt. "We may have sensed it because we're at the bottom of a canyon." Rick looked around, and then back at her with a wry smile. "I'm surprised you didn't fling yourself into my arms."

"We actresses are made of sterner stuff," she said, tossing his words from days ago back at him.

He stifled a laugh. "We made the ground move."

"It was a truck rumbling by!"

"My motorcycle sounds like an earthquake, but an earthquake is just…a truck rumbling by?" he teased.

"Well, it's not us making the ground move, much as you have faith in your superpowers!"

Rick laughed and then glanced around again. "This earthquake didn't seem like a strong one, but you might want to rethink your position on my rocking your world."

"Your ego wouldn't have it any other way?" she asked archly.

"Exactly. Good follow-up, you're learning." He glanced down at her impractical footwear. "Need a hand…or a lift?"

She raised her chin. "No, thanks."

He doubted she'd thank him if he said she looked adorable. "You know, if you left one of those shoes behind…"

"A frog would find it?"

"Some of us are princes in disguise—isn't that how the story goes?"

"Well, this princess is saving herself," she said as she walked past him, head held high, "and not kissing any more frogs!"

Six

The Armani suit was fine, but Rick drew the line at a manicure. He did his own nails, thanks.

In his opinion, premieres and award ceremonies were an evil to be endured, which was another reason he liked his low-profile, low-key existence. Tonight at least was for a good cause—the Ring of Hope Gala to Benefit Children's Charities.

The fund-raiser also explained why Chiara's spacious den was a hub of activity on a Saturday afternoon. The room was usually a quiet oasis, with long windows, beige upholstery and dark wood furniture. Not now, however.

Chiara sat in the makeup chair. Someone was doing her hair, and another person was applying polish to her nails, and all the while Chiara was chatting with Odele. A fashion designer's intern had dropped off two gowns earlier, and at some point, Chiara would slip into one of them, assisted by plenty of double-sided tape and other tricks of the Hollywood magic trade.

Rick figured this amounted to multitasking. Something women were renowned for, and men like him apparently were terrible at—when the reality was probably that men just preferred to do their own nails.

Suddenly Odele frowned at Chiara. "Have you gone through your normal skincare regimen?"

"Yes."

Rick almost laughed. For him, a regimen meant a grueling workout at the gym to get ready for stunts on his next film. It didn't apply to fluffy skincare pampering.

Odele rolled her eyes. "I imagine you raided the kitchen cabinets for sugar and coconut oil, and threw in some yogurt for one of your crazy DIY beauty treatments."

From her chair, Chiara arched her eyebrows, which had been newly plucked. "Of course."

Rick studied those finely arched brows. He hadn't known there was such a thing as threading, and especially not applied to eyebrows. He was a Martian on planet Venus here. Still, he could understand that for an actress like Chiara, whose face was part of her trade, the right look was everything. Subtle changes or enhancements could impact her ability to express emotional nuances.

His gaze moved to Chiara's mouth. Their interlude in the exercise room still weighed on him. She'd been so damn responsive. If she hadn't put a stop to things, he would have taken her right there on the weight bench. In fact, it had been all he could do to keep a cool head the past few days. If it hadn't been for work on the movie set and coming back exhausted after a fourteen-hour day...

Odele sighed. "You're the bane of my existence, Chiara. You could be the face of a cosmetics and skincare line. You're throwing away millions."

"My homemade concoctions work fine," Chiara responded.

"You make your own products?" Rick asked bemusedly.

Chiara shrugged. "I started when I was a teenager and didn't have a dime to my name, and I saw no reason to give it up. I use natural items like avocado."

"Me, too," Rick joked. "But I eat them as part of my strength-training routine."

Chiara peered at him. "I could test the green stuff on your face. You might benefit."

Rick made a mock gesture warding her off. "No, thanks. I'm best friends with my soap."

"Not everyone is blessed with your creamy complexion, Chiara," Odele put in. "Have a little sympathy for the rest of us who could use expensive professional help."

The hairstylist and manicurist stepped away, and Chiara stood, still wrapped in her white terry robe. "Well, time to get dressed."

Rick smiled. "Don't let me stop you."

Odele steamed toward him like a little tugboat pulling Chiara's ship to safe harbor. "We'll call you when we need you."

He shrugged. "More or less explains my role."

Without waiting for further encouragement, he stepped out of the room. For the next half hour, he made somewhat good use of his time by checking his cell phone and catching up on business. Finally, Odele opened the door and motioned him into the den again.

Rick stepped back into the room…and froze, swallowing hard.

Chiara was wearing a one-shoulder gown with a short train. The slit went all the way up one thigh, and the deep red fabric complemented her complexion. She had the ethereal quality of, well, a fairy-tale princess naturally.

"I can't decide which gown," she said.

"The one you're wearing looks good to me."

He knew what the big minefields were, of course. *Do I look fat in this dress?* The automatic answer was *no.* Maybe even *hell, no.* Still, he was ill-equipped for the bombshell that was Chiara Feran—sex poured into a gown.

"You look spectacular," he managed.

She beamed. "I'm wearing a Brazilian designer. I have a platform, and I want to use it."

He knew what *he* wanted.

He'd like nothing better than to swing Chiara into his arms and head for the bedroom. He wasn't particular about *where* frankly, but he didn't want to scandalize her entourage. And if Odele was tipped off, she would be on the phone with Melody Banyon of *WE Magazine* in no time to report his and Chiara's relationship had become serious—never mind that it was make-believe.

Still, the evening was young, and Chiara's manager wouldn't be here at its close...

Flashbulbs went off around them in dizzying bursts of light. The paparazzi were out in full force for this red-carpet event. Chiara gave her practiced smile, crossed one leg in front of the other and tilted her head, giving the photographers her best side.

Her one-shoulder silk organza gown had a deep slit revealing her leg to the upper thigh. It was a beautiful but safe choice for an awards show. Invisible tape ensured everything stayed in place and she didn't have a wardrobe malfunction. Her hair was loose, and her jewelry was limited to chandelier earrings and a diamond bracelet.

The Ring of Hope Gala to Benefit Children's Charities was being held at The Beverly Hilton Hotel. The hotel's sixteen-thousand-foot International Ballroom could seat hundreds—and did for the Golden Globe Awards and other big Hollywood events. Soon she and Rick would be inside, along with dozens of other actors and celebrities.

Rick's hand was at the small of her back—a warm, possessive imprint. It was for the benefit of the cameras, of course, but the reason didn't matter. He made her aware of her femininity. She'd never been so attuned to a man before.

Despite the presence of plenty of well-known actors tonight, Chiara saw women casting Rick lingering looks full of curiosity and interest. He had a blatant sex appeal that was all unpolished male...

Chiara put a break on her wayward thoughts—aware there were dozens of eyes upon them. Not only were bulbs constantly flashing, but the press kept calling out to them.

"Chiara, look this way!"

"Who's the new guy, Chiara?"

"Can you tell us about your gown?"

"Who's the mystery man?"

Chiara curved her lips and called back, "We met on the set of *Pegasus Pride*."

"Is it true he's a stuntman?"

She cast Rick a sidelong look, and he returned it with a lingering one of his own. She could almost believe he was enraptured for real...

"I don't know," she murmured, searching Rick's face. "Do you know some stunts, honey?"

"Not for the red carpet," he said, smiling back. "Maybe I should practice."

Ha. In her opinion, he was doing just fine with his *publicity stunt* for the red carpet. He was *too* believable in the role of boyfriend.

She knew what the headlines would say, of course. *Chiara Feran Makes Debut with New Man.* She and Rick had given their interview to *WE Magazine*, but every media outlet wanted their own story.

Chiara smiled for another few moments. Then she linked hands with Rick and moved out of the spotlight so the next prey—uh, *celebrity*—could take her place. She knew how these things worked.

She and Rick walked into the Hilton, where sanity prevailed in contrast to the paparazzi and fans outside. They followed the crowd toward the International Ballroom. Fortunately she didn't cross paths with anyone she knew well. She wasn't sure if she was up for further discussion of her ultimate accessory—namely, Rick.

When they reached their table, she sighed with relief. *So far, so good.*

"Rick, sugar!"

Chiara turned and spotted an actress she wasn't well-acquainted with but whose name she'd come across more than a few times. *Isabel Lanier.*

She'd never heard Rick's name said in the same breath as *sugar* before. In her opinion, *spice* was more appropriate.

"Wow, I haven't seen you in ages!" Isabel said—and though she addressed Rick, she directed her crystalline blue gaze to Chiara. "And you're one half of an item, too, I hear."

"Isabel, this is—"

"Chiara Feran," Chiara finished for him.

She assessed the other woman. Isabel Lanier had a reputation in Hollywood, and there wasn't enough Botox in LA to make it pretty. She'd slept with directors to land supporting roles. She'd broken up a costar's marriage by having an affair with him during filming. And she'd been named in a lawsuit involving back rent on a house in the Hollywood Hills.

Isabel looked her over in turn, and then, directing her gaze to Rick, murmured, "I'm so glad you've moved on, sugar, and to another actress, too. No bad feelings, hmm?"

Rick seemed to tense, but then Chiara wondered whether she was imagining it.

Isabel fluttered her mascara-heavy eyelashes. "I'd love to talk to you about—"

"Isabel, it was a surprise running into you. Glad you're well."

The dismissal on Rick's part was polite but unmistakable.

Chiara wondered about his past tie to Isabel. It gave her a bad feeling—though, of course, not jealousy. What had Rick been thinking? Isabel? *Really?* The woman's reputation followed her like a trail of discarded clothing in a tacky Vegas hotel room.

Isabel gave them a searching look, and then nodded as if reaching a conclusion. "It's time I got back to my date."

"Hal?" Rick inquired sardonically.

Isabel tossed her head, her smile too bright. "Oh, sugar, you know better." She flashed her hand and a ring caught the light. "But this time, I did find one who is for keeps."

"Congratulations."

The smile stayed on Isabel's lips but her eyes were sharp. "Thank you."

When the other woman moved off, Chiara turned to Rick. "Should I ask?"

"Will you be able to stop yourself?"

"Do you date all your leading ladies?"

"In Isabel's case, it was more her trying to hook up with me. Misguidedly, as it turned out."

Chiara raised her eyebrows.

"Isabel is the reason that I don't get involved with starlets. They're trouble."

"Men are trouble."

"Finally, a topic that we agree on," he quipped. "The opposite sex is trouble."

Chiara shrugged. "Isabel Lanier seems an odd choice for you."

Chiara definitely wasn't jealous. The irony wasn't lost on her, though. Usually her dates were the ones having to contend with overeager male admirers. Now the shoe was on the other foot—sort of.

"Possessive?" Rick asked, lips quirking, as if he'd read her mind.

"Don't be silly," Chiara retorted.

"It's not like you to get territorial, but I like it."

"So what is the connection between you and Isabel Lanier?" she tried again.

Rick regarded her for a moment. "Isabel made a play for me in front of some photographers. Unfortunately her boyfriend at the time was also a good friend of mine. End of friendship."

"Why would she do that?"

Rick gave her a penetrating look. "Fame, public image, to make Hal jealous. You know, all the likely ulterior motives."

She didn't want to dwell on their own ulterior motives right now.

"Shall we sit down?" Rick asked.

She felt compelled to go on. "If you were more high profile, the organizers here would have made sure your path didn't cross Isabel's, and that you were seated on opposite sides of the ballroom."

"Fortunately I'm not. High profile, that is."

"But I am." Chiara made a mental note to put the word out that she and Isabel should be kept apart—at least until her "relationship" with Rick came to an end.

Rick pulled out a chair for her, and she sat down. As Rick turned to acknowledge a waiter, Isabel fished the cell phone out of her clutch and typed a quick text to Odele. No time like the present to make sure a viper stayed in her tank, she thought, her mind traveling back to Isabel.

After that, the evening passed quickly and painlessly. The master of ceremonies was a well-known comedian, and he drew regular laughs from the crowd, who dined on butterfly salmon pâté with caviar and peppered chateaubriand with port wine glacé.

Before long, Chiara found herself heading home with Rick. She'd never had a live-in significant other, and in the past, it had been easy enough to say goodbye at the end of a date. Not this time, however. *Awkward.*

When they entered the hushed silence of her foyer, she faced Rick. She reminded herself that she held the cards here. She was the celebrity. This was *her* house. And he, for all intents and purposes, was *her* employee, thanks to Odele.

Still, it was of little help when faced with Rick's overwhelming masculinity.

He was tall and broad, and all evening she'd been ignoring how he filled out his tux. Should she be surprised he even owned one?

Rick quirked his lips. "I guess this is the part where I kiss you good-night—" he glanced past her to the stairs "—except I'm staying here." His gaze came back to hers, and he looked at her with a slow deliberateness.

All of a sudden, she was searching for air. They hadn't been this close since their encounter in the exercise room, and she'd vowed it was an experience that would never, ever be repeated.

But the memory of how easily he'd aroused her— her body tightening and then finding blessed release—played havoc with her senses and scruples right now.

He bent his head, and said in a low voice, "It would aid in believability."

There was no need for him to elaborate. If he kissed her…if he excited her…if they became lovers…

Yes…no. She mentally shook her head.

He looked down at her gown, and she felt his gaze everywhere—on her breasts, her hips and lower…

"Do you need help with that dress?" he muttered, his eyes half-lidded. "There's no Odele here, no designer's assistant or fashion stylist."

Didn't she know it. They were alone, and the quiet of the night and the empty house surrounded them.

The only illumination was the dim light that she'd left on in the foyer.

Chiara cleared her throat. "You did well tonight for an agoraphobic stuntman."

"Isn't this the time in the movie for a love scene?" he teased.

She tried gamely for her typical maneuver. She did *outrage* really well. "This isn't a movie and we're not—"

"Actors," he finished for her. "I know."

He took her hand and drew her near. Another smile teased his lips. "That's what's going to make this so great. No pretending."

She swallowed. "I don't know how not to pretend."

The brutal honesty escaped her before she could help herself.

"Just feel. Go with your instincts."

"Like method acting?"

"Like real life." He settled his hands and massaged her shoulders. "Relax. We stuntmen are not so bad."

"Are you the baddest of the bunch?" she asked, her voice husky.

His smile widened. "Want to find out if I'm the Big Bad Wolf?"

"Sorry, wrong fairy tale again."

She could feel the heat and energy coming off him even though only his hands touched her. She was attuned to *everything* about him. As an actress, she was trained to observe the slightest facial sign, the subtlest inflection of voice, the intention behind a touch. But with Rick, she quivered with sensation approaching a sixth sense.

Slowly he raised her chin, and her gaze met his.

They'd been working up to this moment ever since the exercise room, and she saw in his eyes that he knew it, too.

He searched her face and then, focusing on her mouth, he brushed her lips with his.

She parted for him on an indrawn sigh, touched her tongue to his and twined her arms around his neck. She needed this, too, she admitted, and for tonight at least she couldn't think of a reason to deny herself.

He settled his hands on her waist, and she felt the press of his arousal. He deepened the kiss, and she met him, not holding back. Her evening clutch slipped from her limp hand and hit the ground with a small *thump*.

He broke the kiss, only to trail his mouth, whisper-soft, across her jaw and to her temple.

"Rick…"

"Chiara."

"I…"

"This isn't the time to start one of your arguments."

"About what?"

"About anything."

He nuzzled the side of her neck, and she angled her head to afford him better access. She fastened her hands on his biceps in order to anchor herself, and the hard muscle under her fingers reminded her that he was built…and right now primed to mate with her.

Chiara felt that last realization to her core, even as Rick's lips sent delicious shivers down her spine.

One of his hands shifted lower and settled on her exposed thigh. She felt the caress of his slightly callused fingers.

He kissed the shell of her ear, and then whispered, "Your dress has been giving me a thrill all evening."

"Oh?" she managed.

"The slit is so high…playing peekaboo all the way up…making me wonder whether this time I'll get a glimpse…"

She gave a throaty laugh. "I'm not commando. I don't take those kinds of risks."

His hand moved lower, slid under the slit and covered her. "Oh, yeah? But I want you to go on all kinds of adventures with me. Let me show you, baby…"

Chiara's eyes closed and her head fell back as Rick's finger slipped inside her and the pad of his thumb brushed her in a wicked dance. Her lips parted. *Oh, my.* They hadn't even made it past the inside of her front door and all she wanted to do was strip for him and let him take her against the hard wall of the foyer, pounding into her until she wept with the pure ecstasy of it, her legs wrapped around him and holding him close.

"Ah, Chiara." His voice sounded rough with arousal as he nipped and nibbled along her jaw. "So hot. There's nothing cold about you."

His words wrapped around her like a warm caress. She'd worked all her life to get her walls up and, most of all, be independent and succeed. But with Rick, her defenses came crashing down, and in their place rushed in powerful need.

Rick snaked his free hand beneath the one-shoulder bodice of her gown and cupped her breast. He kneaded her soft flesh and she peaked for him.

A moan escaped her.

"I should have stuck around earlier tonight so I'd know how you got into this gown, and how to get you out," he muttered.

A laugh caught in her throat, but then the buzz of a cell phone interrupted the mood like the beam of car headlights slicing through the night.

It took a few moments for Chiara to clear her head and get oriented. And then she flushed. She and Rick had gone from zero to sixty in minutes, and any longer...

As her phone continued to buzz from the inside of her clutch on the floor, she pulled away from Rick, and he dropped his hands and stepped back.

"You don't have to answer it," he said roughly.

"It's Odele. I can tell from the ringtone." She started to bend down, but Rick was faster and retrieved the clutch for her.

"You don't have to answer it," Rick commented, his voice edged with frustration.

Flustered and still aroused, Chiara gathered her scattered thoughts. "She's used to having her calls answered. I—I've got to take this. I've...got to go."

"Of course." His expression was sardonic, knowing, and he raked his hand through his hair. "I'm guessing it's time for another cold shower."

Turning away from Rick to regain her composure, she hit the answer button. "Odele, hello?"

"Hello, sweetie. How are you? Did you have a fine evening?"

"Yes, of course," she answered as she hurried up the stairs. "What can I do for you, Odele?"

"I'm responding to your request, hon."

For a moment, Chiara was confused, but then she remembered her text to Odele earlier in the evening.

"From what I could see on TV, you and Mr. Stuntman were doing an excellent job at your first public appearance together. But then I got your message about keeping you and Isabel Lanier separated at future social events. Did something happen that I'm not aware of?"

Chiara didn't know whether to be relieved or frustrated. If not for Odele's untimely—or rather, timely—call, she'd have been moments away from inviting Rick to follow her to the bedroom. A mistake that she would have regretted.

"Not that I don't have sympathy," Odele went on in her trademark raspy voice. "Isabel Lanier reeks of tacky perfume, and her manager is worse."

Chiara smiled weakly. Leave it to Odele to be competitive with even Isabel's snarky manager.

"So, honey, are you going to tell me what the story is, or make me guess? I have my sources, you know."

Chiara lowered her voice even as she reached the privacy of her bedroom and flipped on the light. "Rick and Isabel were involved at one point."

"Really?" The word was a long, drawn-out drawl.

"Well, not really." Chiara dropped her clutch on the vanity table. "She sort of threw herself at him in a publicity stunt and that was the end of his friendship with her then boyfriend."

"Damn it, I knew her manager was cunning."

"It takes one to know one, Odele."

"Okay, all right," her manager responded grumpily. "Now that I've got the details, I'll put the word out about Isabel and file away the information for any future events that I book you for."

"You're a doll, Odele."

"Oh, stop," her manager rasped. "I'm a barracuda in a town infested with sharks."

When she ended the call with Odele, Chiara sighed. The conversation had let sanity back in. She couldn't get involved with Rick. Sweet heaven, she didn't even like him. She *couldn't* like him.

Too bad she was having an increasingly hard time remembering why.

Seven

Welsdale was a quaint New England town with brick buildings dotting the main streets and colorful homes lining the back roads.

Chiara could hardly believe she was here except that Odele had, of course, loved Rick's idea for an appearance on his mother's cooking show. Before Chiara had caught her breath, she and Rick had been on an early flight from Los Angeles to Boston.

She supposed it was just as well. Ever since the Ring of Hope Gala last weekend, she'd done her best to keep Rick at arm's length. Only a long couple of days on set had saved her. She'd collapsed into bed, exhausted, late at night.

From the airport, where Rick had a car in long-term parking, they drove to Welsdale and then, after no more than twenty minutes on oak-lined roads, to a stunning home on the outskirts of town. Rick had mentioned that his parents were hosting a small party at their house.

The elder Serenghettis lived in a Mediterranean-style mansion with a red-tile roof and white walls. Set amidst beautiful landscaping, the house greeted visitors with a stone fountain at the center of a circular drive.

Chiara didn't know what she had expected, except perhaps a humbler abode. Clearly she'd been wrong in her assumptions. Rick came from an established family and a comfortable background, unlike her.

When they stepped inside, Rick stretched out his arms and joked, "Welcome to the Serenghetti family reunion."

Chiara blinked. "They're all here?"

"We like to support Mom."

Oh, sweet heaven. She wasn't prepared for this. The gathering was larger than she'd expected, and it seemed that assorted Serenghettis were sprinkled among the crowd.

There'd be no Feran family reunion, of course. Or if there were, it would be at a Las Vegas gaming table, where she'd be settling her father's debts.

People were standing around chatting in the family room and adjacent living room, and she noticed in particular how two of the men were as attractive as Rick. It appeared the Serenghetti men came in one variety only: drop-dead gorgeous.

"Come on," Rick said, cupping her elbow. "I'll introduce you."

As they approached, one of the two men glanced at them and then came forward. "Ah, the prodigal son returning to the fold…"

"Stuff it, Jordan." Rick's tone was good-natured—as if he was used to being ribbed.

Jordan appeared unabashed and gave Chiara an openly curious look. "Well, this time you've outdone yourself. Mom will be pleased. But how you managed to convince a beautiful actress that you've got the goods, I'll never know." He held out his hand. "Hi, I'm Jordan Serenghetti, Rick's better-looking brother."

"Which one of us was a body double for *People*'s Sexiest Man Alive?" Rick retorted mildly.

"Which one is featured in an underwear ad on a billboard in Times Square?" Jordan returned.

"Nice to meet you," Chiara jumped in with a light laugh. "I've been putting up with his humor—" she indicated Rick "—for days. Now I see it's a family trait."

"Yes, but I'm younger than Rick and our older brother, Cole, so I like to say our parents achieved perfection only the third time around."

When Rick raised his eyebrows, Chiara laughed again. It was good to see Rick getting back some of his own.

Rick's gaze went to the arched entrance to the family room, and Chiara spotted an attractive woman with honey-blond hair caught in a ponytail, a nice figure showcased in tights and a short-sleeved athletic shirt. Unlike many women in Hollywood, she seemed unaware of her beauty, sporting a fresh-faced natural look with little makeup.

"Your nemesis is here," Rick murmured.

Jordan followed his brother's gaze. "Heaven help us."

At Chiara's inquiring look, Rick elaborated. "Serafina is related to us by marriage. She's Cole's wife's cousin. She also happens to be the one woman under the sun Jordan can't charm."

Jordan wore an unguarded look that said he was attracted like a bee to nectar—and befuddled by the feeling. Chiara hid a smile. She suspected that like her, Jordan lived in a world with plenty of artifice— big-time sports likely resembled Hollywood that way—and Serafina was a breath of fresh air.

Serafina was something different, and Jordan appeared at a loss as to how to deal with her. Relative? Friend? Lover? Maybe he couldn't make up his mind—and it wasn't only his choice to make, either.

"Excuse me," Jordan announced. "Fun just walked in."

"Jordan," Rick said warningly.

"What?" his brother responded as he stepped away.

"Just make sure that while you're getting a rise out of our newest in-law, you don't come in for a pounding yourself."

Jordan flashed a quick grin. "I'm counting on it."

Chiara watched Serafina's eyes narrow as she noticed Jordan step toward her. It seemed as if Jordan wasn't the only one who was aware of someone else's every move…

Then Chiara quashed a sudden self-deprecatory grimace. She couldn't judge Serafina. She herself was attuned to Rick's every gesture.

At that moment, the other attractive man Chiara had spotted earlier approached.

"Hi, I'm Cole Serenghetti," he said, holding out his hand.

"Chiara Feran," she responded, shaking hands.

She could tell on a moment's acquaintance that Cole was the serious brother.

Unlike Jordan and Rick, Cole's eyes were more hazel than green. Still, the family resemblance was strong. But Chiara noticed that Cole sported a scar on his cheek.

A beautiful woman walked up to them, and Cole put his arm around her. She had the most translucent brown eyes that Chiara had ever seen, and masses of brown hair that fell in waves and curls past her shoulders.

"This is my wife, Marisa," Cole said, looking affectionately at the woman beside him. "Sweet pea, I'm sure you've heard of Chiara Feran."

"I loved your movie *Three Nights in Paris*," Marisa gushed, "and I follow you online."

Chiara smiled. "It's good to meet you. So you like romantic comedies?"

"I adore them." Marisa threw a teasing look at her husband. "Though it's hard to get Cole here to watch them with me."

"Ouch." Cole adopted a mock-wounded expression. "Hey, I'm just showing family loyalty to Rick for his adventure flicks."

"A great excuse," Marisa parried before turning back to Chiara. "You aren't filming a romantic comedy now, are you?"

Chiara sighed. "Unfortunately no." Unless she counted the banter that she had going on with Rick offscreen. "Blame Hollywood. Action movies bring in the big bucks at the box office."

Marisa made a sympathetic sound.

"You're a woman after my own heart," Chiara said.

"I've had my tenth grade students watch you in the film adaptation of *Another Song at Dawn*," Marisa added enthusiastically. "I've taught here in Welsdale."

Chiara warmed to the other woman. "I'm so glad. That's the nicest compliment—"

"Anyone's ever paid you?" Rick finished for her.

Cole cast Rick a droll look. "Quite the romantic boyfriend, aren't you?"

Chiara flushed. "I meant the best professional praise."

Cole and his wife just laughed.

"Cole's gotten better with sharing warm thoughts since we've gotten married," Marisa added, throwing a playful look at her husband, "but I'm still not finding little heart drawings in my lunchbox."

Chiara envied Cole and Marisa's obvious connection. In contrast, she and Rick pushed each other's buttons. Then she reminded herself there was no *her and Rick.* They had a fake relationship for the benefit of the press.

When Cole and Marisa excused themselves, another woman approached, and Chiara again saw a resemblance to Rick.

"Chiara, this is my younger sister, Mia," Rick said.

Mia was slender and lovely, with arresting almond-shaped green eyes. She could have qualified as a model or actress herself.

"I wish I could say Rick has told me a lot about you," Mia quipped, "but I'd be lying."

"Family," Rick muttered. "Who needs enemies?"

Mia tossed her brother a droll look that made Chiara smile.

"Rick mentioned you're a designer," Chiara said.

"He did?"

"I'd love to see some of your creations."

"I'm based in New York."

"Do you have something that Chiara could toss on for an appearance on Mom's cooking show?" Rick prompted.

When Mia rolled her eyes, Chiara held back a grin.

"Leave it to my brother to give me the professional opportunity of a lifetime, and no fair warning."

"Hey," Rick said, holding up his hands, "I did tell you to bring a trunk of stuff to show a friend of mine."

"Yeah, but you didn't say who!"

"Don't you read any of the celebrity glossies or supermarket tabloids?" Rick countered. "I'm dating one of the hottest actresses around."

Chiara felt a wave of heat at the word *hottest.*

"How am I supposed to know what's true and what isn't?" Mia responded. "It's a good thing I know my way around a needle and thread for a little nip and tuck if necessary."

"I'm not that thin," Chiara chimed in.

"Yeah, she has the appetite of a lumberjack," Rick agreed jokingly. "I should know. I've carried her out of exploding buildings and onto a helicopter with one hand."

"Hilarious, Rick," Mia said. "Next you'll be telling us that you have real superpowers."

Rick arched an eyebrow. "Ask Chiara."

Chiara flushed again. The last thing she wanted to do was discuss Rick's prowess—sexual or otherwise—with his siblings.

When Chiara didn't immediately reply, Mia laughed. "I guess you got your answer, Rick."

An older woman came bustling over, clapping her hands. "*Cari, scusatemi.* I'm sorry, I was speaking on the phone with my producers."

Rick's face lightened. "Don't worry, Mom. We're all good here. Just introducing Chiara to everybody."

Rick's mother clasped her hands together. "I'm Camilla. *Benvenuti.*"

"Thank you for the welcome, Mrs. Serenghetti," Chiara said.

"Camilla, please. You are doing me a huge *favore.*"

"She mixes Italian and English like they're flour and water," Rick said in a low voice. "Interrupt at your own risk."

"Now, Chiara—what a lovely name! You are Italian and Brazilian, no?"

She nodded her head.

"You are a celebrity, yes? And beautiful, too, no?"

"Um…"

"Basta, così." Camilla nodded her head approvingly. "It is enough. You are doing me a huge *favore*. Anything else will be extra filling in the cannoli, no?"

"Mrs. Serenghetti—"

"Camilla, please. Do you want me to demonstrate a recipe to you on the show, or—" Camilla brightened hopefully "—you have one to share?"

"Actually I do." Chiara had been thinking about the show on the plane ride. She didn't want to disappoint. It had nothing to do with Rick, but rather her own high standards and integrity, she told herself. "I used to visit relatives in Brazil when I was growing up. Italian food is very popular there."

Camilla beamed.

"Brazilian barbecue—" Chiara began.

"Churrascaria, sì."

"—is well-known, but we also have *galeteria*. It's chicken and usually an all-you-can-eat pasta and salad. So I would like to make a pasta dish that sounds Italian, but was really popularized by the Italian immigrant community in Brazil. *Cappelletti alla romanesca.*"

"Perfetto." Camilla nodded approvingly.

Mia linked arms with her mother. "Excuse us while I get Mom's opinion on how to finish the tagliatelle salad."

When his female relatives had departed, Rick turned to Chiara with a bemused expression. "I'm impressed. Have you actually made this dish before?"

"Please." Chiara gave him a long-suffering look. "Do I look Brazilian and Italian to you?"

"Yes, but—"

"Trust me." The words were out of her mouth before she could stop them.

"Isn't that my line?" he mocked.

She felt the heat rise in her cheeks and turned away.

"Rick!"

Chiara spotted an older version of Rick coming toward them.

"Brace yourself," Rick murmured. "You have yet to meet the most colorful member of the family. Serg Serenghetti."

Oh, dear.

"So the prodigal son has returned."

"Wrong script, Dad," Rick quipped. "This is *The Son Also Rises*."

Serg Serenghetti fastened his eyes on Chiara. "What do you see in this guy?"

Chiara gave a weak smile.

"How do you know about us?" Rick retorted, addressing his father.

"I read *WE Magazine*," Serg grumbled. "Same as everyone else. Your mother leaves copies lying around." Serg lowered his brows. "And with my recovery, I have plenty of time to surf the internet for news about my wayward children."

Rick looked at Chiara and jerked a finger in his father's direction. "Do you believe he knows about surfing? He's keeping up with those teenagers that make action flicks such blockbusters at the box office."

As Rick poked fun at his father, his tone was laced with affection.

Serg grumbled again. "I've known a lot about a lot for a lot longer than you've been around, but all I get is guff from the young pups."

Rick pulled out a chair, and Serg sank into it.

"He's still recovering from a stroke," Rick murmured for her benefit.

Oh. Chiara felt a tug at her heartstrings. Beneath the bluster, the affection between father and son sounded loud and clear. In contrast, her relationship with her father was a distant echo.

Chiara realized that with the Serenghettis, she was in for something new and different from her own experience. And as she settled into a conversation with Serg, she realized that might not be such a bad thing—except for the fact that meeting his family made Rick even more likable and attractive, and she was already in danger of succumbing to him…

Rick couldn't believe his eyes, but then he should have known Chiara would be a natural in front of the cameras—even on Camilla Serenghetti's cooking show.

He was also tense. He wanted this episode to boost ratings for his mother, but he had little idea about Chiara's cooking skills, let alone how they'd play out on

television. And he also wanted Chiara and his mother
to get along.

So far so good.

"The reason I'm not wearing an apron," Chiara
said brightly into the camera, "is because this outfit
is too scrumptious to cover up." She gestured at her
V-neck berry-colored top with clever draping, the
cream trousers underneath barely visible above the
kitchen counter. "It's courtesy of Camilla's daughter,
Mia Serenghetti, whose clothes are mouth-watering."

Camilla laughed, and because she sat next to him
in the audience, Rick could tell his sister looked
amused.

"I guess Camilla is not the only talented one in
the family."

"*Grazie tanto*, Chiara *bellissima*," his mother said.

"*Prego.*" Chiara acknowledged the thanks and
then dumped prosciutto in a blender before smiling
at the studio audience. "I sometimes prefer an elec-
tronic device to hand-chopping. Goes faster, too."

As she scanned the buttons on the blender, Rick
realized something was wrong and started to rise
from his front-row seat.

Chiara pressed a button, and prosciutto pieces
started flying everywhere.

Chiara yelped, and Camilla covered her mouth
with her hands. The audience exploded in shocked
laughter.

Rick stared, and then sank back into his seat.

Chiara quickly pressed another button to turn off

the blender, and then she and Camilla stared at each other…before dissolving into peals of laughter.

"Oops." Chiara looked into the camera and shrugged, a teasing smile on her face. "Next time I'll remember to put the top on the blender first. But first let's get this cleaned up."

Moments later, after help from behind-the-scenes staff, Chiara raised a wineglass, and she and Camilla toasted each other.

Rick watched, fascinated by the interplay between the two women. Looking around him, he realized everyone else was entertained, as well.

After that, Chiara proceeded to prepare the cappelletti recipe without another hitch. She chopped more prosciutto, by hand this time, and added it to a shallow pan containing peas, mushrooms and a light cream sauce. With a saucy look, she added a touch of *vino* from the open wine bottle, and said with a wink, "Do try this at home, but not too much."

His mother laughed, and then both she and Chiara took more sips from their wineglasses.

Rick couldn't imagine what they were both thinking, but when Chiara motioned for his father, Serg, to join them from the audience, Rick knew things were only going to get more interesting. His father was a character, but this was the first time Serg had been so public since his stroke.

Rick made to help his father out of his seat, but Serg just batted his hand away.

"Bah!" Serg said, doing a comical rendition of a

grumpy old man even though he had the grin of an eager fan.

"I hear Camilla's husband, Serg, knows his way around wine," Chiara announced. "Perhaps he can suggest a vintage to pair with my dish."

"I'd be happy to," Serg replied as he climbed the two steps to the stage. "It's not every day that my son brings home a beautiful actress."

Rick suppressed an embarrassed groan. His and Chiara's pretend relationship had just gotten a major advertising boost from his father. Odele would be overjoyed.

When Serg reached the stage, he sampled the cappelletti dish from a plate Camilla handed to him. After taking a moment to savor, he declared, "Bianco di Custoza, Verdicchio or Pinot Bianco."

Chiara beamed. "Thank you so much for the wine suggestions, Serg."

Serg winked at the audience. "You know I'm Italian, so I suggest Italian wines. I like them on the dry side, but you can pair this dish with a lighter Chardonnay if you like."

Getting the signal from a producer offscreen, Camilla addressed the camera in order to wrap up the show. *"All prossima volta.* Till next time, *buon appetito."*

As the show's support staff approached to remove Camilla's and Chiara's mics, Serg returned to his seat.

"Good job, Dad," Rick remarked with a smile. "I didn't know you had it in you."

He was still trying to process Chiara's interaction

with his parents on camera. It was like she'd known them forever, it had been so natural.

"Bah!" Serg said, though his expression again belied his grumpiness. "Don't be jealous I was the one called on stage by a beautiful woman. You've got to work it, Rick."

"And a star is born," Rick replied with dry humor to his sister, who gave a knowing smile.

"Do you want my autograph?" Serg chortled, picking up his sweater from his seat as Mia moved to help him.

Rick stepped off to the side, and when Chiara approached, minutes later, he remarked, "That was quite a scene-stealing performance."

"It's why I'm an in-demand actress."

She looked sexy in Mia's designs, and he liked her even more for lending her celebrity to help his family.

"So it was all planned?"

"Planned? Like reading lines?" She shook her head. "No. More like improv and stand-up comedy."

"It worked."

"I hope the show's ratings reflect it." She shrugged. "Viewers want drama and action. Or maybe I just think that because I've been doing too many adventure movies."

"Hey—" he chucked her under the chin "—that's how you met a hunky stuntman who's given you a new lease on life in the press."

"Oh, yes, the media." She made a disgruntled sound that he didn't expect. "Of course, I have to attend to my public persona."

He tucked his hands in his denim pockets—because the urge to comfort and, even more, get closer to her, was overwhelming. "So who is the real Chiara Feran? Odele mentioned a few details about your childhood and parents."

She sighed, and there was a flash of pain. "My mother was in some ways a typical stage mother, but in other ways, she wasn't. She had thwarted dreams of being a star, so she was ambitious for me."

"Things didn't work out for her?"

"Well, she had some modest success in Brazil, so she went to Hollywood. But the Portuguese accent didn't help when it came to acting roles. Who knows what would have happened if she'd stayed in South America."

Curious, Rick asked, "Your mother didn't want more kids?"

Chiara sobered. "No. Her marriage broke up, and I was enough for her to handle as a single parent living far from her family in Brazil. Plus, I was her spitting image in many ways, so she already had a Mini-Me. She died a few years ago, and I still miss her a lot. I have mixed feelings about my childhood, but I loved her with my whole heart. She did the best she could in raising me."

Rick was starting to understand—a lot. Chiara's upbringing couldn't have been more different from his own. While he'd been tossing around a football in the backyard with his siblings, she was probably being prepped and groomed for a chance to appear in a national commercial or catalog.

"Your mother should think of doing a food blog," Chiara commented, changing the subject. "She needs to think of branching out and building the Camilla Serenghetti food empire."

"Empire?" he repeated in a sardonic tone. Because while it was one thing for his mother to have a local cooking show, it was another for her to be an empress in the making. Still… "She'll like the way you think, and appreciate the pointers on building a brand."

"Of course. That's what we're about in Hollywood. Building a brand." Chiara looked around. "You, on the other hand, are about wholesomeness, surprisingly enough. Or at least your family is. You come from a nice little town in Massachusetts that's ages away from the Sunset Strip."

"You grew up in Rhode Island, not far from here. You're not so different."

Chiara shook her head. "I'm all about performing these days. The show must go on."

"Whatever the cost?" Rick probed.

Chiara nodded. "Even if the show is a sham."

"And yet, I think of you as real and vital," Rick replied, stepping closer. "And my physical reaction to you definitely is."

She gave a nervous laugh and shook her head. "You must be mistaken. I'm Snow White, remember? A make-believe character."

Rick's lips twitched. He wasn't sure when they had gotten so mixed up. Suddenly *she* was insisting she was a make-believe character, and *he* was arguing the opposite.

One thing was for sure: he was more determined than ever to finish exploring their very real attraction. He'd kept his distance since they'd left Los Angeles, but he wanted her with a need that was getting hard to ignore.

In the now nearly empty television studio, Chiara stood to one side, waiting for assorted Serenghettis to depart. Rick was speaking to his mother and one of her producers, no doubt making sure everything was in order with respect to today's guest appearance.

Chiara was glad for the respite. Minutes ago, her conversation with Rick had devolved into a far more intimate and personal exchange than she'd been prepared for. What had she been thinking?

She'd revealed more about her background and her mother than she'd intended. And then she hadn't been able to keep out the wistfulness when contrasting her circumstances with Rick's own family. *Wholesome. Warm. Loving.* She felt relaxed here, in the embrace of the Serenghettis and away from her problems—the limelight, her father, her would-be stalker...

Still, she'd dodged the very real emotional and sexual currents between her and Rick by making light of the matter. *The show must go on.* She doubted Rick would be satisfied with that response, however. Awareness skated over her skin as she remembered the gleam in his eyes followed by his words: *I think of you as real and vital. And my physical reaction to you definitely is.*

Her resolve to keep him at a distance was weakening, aided by her very real yearning for what he'd had—still had—in comparison: a tight-knit family who cared about each other.

As if on cue, Rick's sister appeared, her face wreathed in a wide smile. "Thank you for the on-air plug, Chiara. You are the perfect model to bring out the best in my designs."

Chiara smiled back and then touched the other woman's arm. "Don't mention it."

"I've never dressed someone so high profile before. You have a great sense of style."

"I owe a lot to my former stylist Emery. But she went off to start her own accessories line, so I'm open to new ideas." Chiara's eyes widened, as an idea struck. "I should connect the both of you. Emery would be a natural complement to your clothing line."

Mia gave a look of wry amusement. "I can see it now—'ME by Mia Emery... Not Your Mom's Everyday.'"

"Perfect." So this was what it might be like to have a sister. Chiara let the wistful feeling wash over her again.

Mia tilted her head. "Rick isn't the only maverick in the family, though he likes to think so. I've abandoned the family construction business and run off to New York to follow the bright lights of fashion."

"You make *maverick* sound like a bad thing. It's not so terrible."

"Not so wicked, you mean?" Mia gave a sly grin. "So Rick's worked his charm on you then?"

Chiara's face warmed. Was it *charm*—or something more? Just a short time ago, she'd have called Rick the least charming man she knew, but somehow her feelings had been changing. Now with his family, she was even more…charmed.

Mia leaned in conspiratorially. "You're beautiful, smart and famous. How did you and Rick wind up together?"

"We…um…" Somehow she couldn't bring herself to lie to Rick's sister, so she finished lamely, "Don't believe everything you read in the press."

What could she say? *We're not really a couple. It's a big fat lie.* Even if she was having increasing trouble remembering that, especially surrounded by the Serenghettis.

"I see," Mia responded, and then nodded as if satisfied. "Well, you two bounce off each other in a charming way. It's as if Rick has met his match."

Even if that were true, it meant one of them was going down for the count…

"You're someone who can't be impressed by his money," Mia added.

What? Chiara mentally shrugged, and said carefully, "I'm not sure how much money Rick has."

Mia laughed. "Neither am I, but after making a killing with his hedge fund, he's got enough to play with."

Hedge fund? Chiara felt her head swim. Rick was a gritty rolling stone of a stuntman as far as she knew. If he had millions, what was he doing…?

"He's a stuntman," she blurted. "He jumps off

buildings, leaps from moving cars…" *And embraces actresses while hanging from a helicopter.*

"And takes big risks with money by betting things are going up or down in value." Mia shrugged. "Same thing."

Chiara froze. Mia made it seem as if Rick was a risk taker—which wasn't far from her gambling father. She'd never seen the similarity, and now she was in a very public relationship with Rick. She needed therapy…and not the kind provided by pretending to talk with a wooden dummy, either. *Sorry, Ruby.*

But even more shockingly, Rick wasn't merely a stuntman, he was—

"*Pegasus Pride* is his baby right now," his sister said.

Chiara blew out a breath and tried to keep her voice steady. "He's got money invested in the film?"

Mia nodded. "You didn't know?"

Nope. Otherwise she'd never have spent her time insulting the boss—the producer of her current film—who could have had her fired any day.

Mia gave a choked laugh. "That's just like Rick. He always wants to keep a low profile." Her eyes suddenly danced. "We're still talking about his favorite childhood Halloween costume. You know, he just tossed a brown paper bag over his head and made cutouts for eyes."

"And the school play?" Chiara nearly squeaked.

"Stage crew, or he'd play the tree, of course."

"Well, he's graduated to leaping from speeding

motorcycles and hanging from airplanes," Chiara replied drily. *And tricking unwary actresses.*

She glanced over at Rick. Why hadn't he told her? She'd thought...they'd... Chiara nearly closed her eyes on a groan.

She *really* needed to talk to him. But not around his family. No, she'd have to wait for the right moment...

Eight

Chiara somehow managed to keep her silence until they were at Rick's place.

At least now she understood why he might be checking his phone all the time. He was a behind-the-scenes Hollywood power player who liked to keep his name out of the press. And perhaps he needed to keep track of his substantial financial investments, too.

When they arrived at his condo, she was impressed all over again. But at least now she was prepared for what she found, unlike when they'd first arrived in Welsdale. The airy space had the stamp of muted luxury: exposed brick, rich leathers, recessed lighting and electronics hidden behind sliding panels of artwork. Nearly floor-to-ceiling windows made the most of the apartment's perch on the top floor of a block of high-priced condos, and Welsdale's evening lights twinkled outside.

How was it possible she'd been in the dark? She'd researched Rick again online after her conversation with Mia, and nothing had come up. He was good at covering his tracks. Except she was on his trail, thanks to his sister.

She sauntered into the muted light of the living room ahead of Rick. He was dressed in slacks and an open-collar navy shirt. A five o'clock shadow made him look even sexier.

Chiara smoothed her hands down the front of her pants. Then, taking a deep breath, she pinned Rick with a steady gaze. "You didn't tell me you're the producer of *Pegasus Pride* as well as doing its stunt work."

When he didn't react, she didn't know whether to stamp her foot or applaud his acting skills.

"Surprise."

"Now is not the time for humor, Serenghetti."

"When is?" He continued to look relaxed.

She placed her hands on her hips. "You misled me."

"You didn't ask. Anyway, does it matter?"

"I never date the boss," she huffed. "I don't want the reputation of being the actress who slept her way to the top."

On the long list of what he'd done wrong, it was one of the lesser of his transgressions, but she was nearly speechless and didn't even know where to begin.

Rick, though, had the poor grace to smile. "Does it help to know I'm only the behind-the-scenes guy? I'm an investor in Blooming Star Productions."

"Why don't you get your mother a cameo in a movie then? She could play herself. A cook with a local television show trying to make it big."

"God help us."

Chiara narrowed her eyes. "And where did you get the money to be the financial backer for a film production company?"

She'd heard it from Mia—and hadn't quite believed it—so she wanted confirmation from the source himself.

He shrugged. "I worked on Wall Street after Boston College and created a hedge fund."

She felt light-headed when he told her this, just as she had at the television studio. How much money were they talking about? Millions? Billions?

As if reading her mind, he said, "I've made a few best-of lists, but I left New York before joining the billionaires' club."

She figured he had serious bank dwarfing that of a run-of-the-mill actress. "It's unheard of to be both a producer and a stuntman!"

"They're not as different as you think. Both involve calculated risks. One with money, the other physically."

His words echoed Mia's earlier. What was this, a Serenghetti press release? Or did Rick and his siblings just think alike?

She should have been able to read the signs and

put them together. They were all there. The expensive car. The apartments on two coasts.

He shrugged again. "I'm a maverick."

"You said you lived in a rental in West Hollywood!"

"Until the house is finished. It's under construction."

"And where is this house?" she asked suspiciously.

"Beverly Hills."

But of course. "Brentwood must seem…quaint to you."

There were plenty of celebrities in her section of LA but it was a little more low-key than the brand-name neighborhoods where tourists flocked—Beverly Hills, Bel Air…

Rick's lips twitched. "Brentwood has its charms, particularly if there's a thatched English cottage… and fairy-tale princess involved."

"She's the kick-ass modern variety," she sniffed—because she should be verbally demolishing him right now for letting her believe he was just an *aw-shucks* stuntman living for the next thrill and its accompanying paycheck.

"Don't I know it." His eyes laughed at her.

"Why would you give up New York, the financial industry and your own hedge fund to go out West to Hollywood?"

He smiled a little, still unflappable. "New challenges. Hollywood is not that different from Wall Street. The studios take major gambles with movies.

Different rules, but the same game. And it's still about trusting your instincts and making money—or not."

"Well, it all makes sense now—" sarcasm crept into her tone "—except for the part where you led me to believe you were a regular Joe."

"Is this our first argument?"

She nearly snorted. "Or our hundredth."

He sauntered closer. "Would it have made a difference if you'd known?"

"You could have hired a stable of bodyguards for me with your bank!"

"Ah," he drawled, "but then I wouldn't have had the pleasure of…your company."

"The joy of sparring with me, you mean? And living in a humble cottage instead of a castle in Beverly Hills?"

He burst out laughing. "I'm paying you enough to live in more than a humble cottage."

"But are you paying me enough to put up with you?"

He gave a sultry smile and reached for her. "I don't know. Let's find out."

She should be mad at him. She *was* angry with him. Still, it didn't matter. The truth was she'd been lured in by the seductive cozy family life of the Serenghettis. She yearned for it. They were miles removed from her existence in Southern California, and the distance wasn't just a matter of geography.

When Rick's lips met hers, Chiara was transported, winging through the clouds as if they were performing another one of their stunts. Exhilaration ran through her, the feeling humming alongside one of safety, family...and coming home.

He molded her to him with his hand on her back, making her feel his need—his desire. She rested her hands on his shoulders, and then, caving, slid her arms around his neck, bringing his head closer.

Rick lifted his head slightly, and muttered against her mouth, "We need props."

She gave a choked laugh. "This is not a film scene."

Rick raised his eyebrows. "You're an actress who's not into role-playing?"

"I like to keep it real. Well, except for this pretending about being a couple that Odele has me doing!"

"Believe me, this is as real and raw as it's going to get."

Awareness shivered through her. "Okay, what if I'm a chilly A-list actress and you're...the help who is intent on seducing me?"

"There's nothing cold about you, Snow," he said, tilting up her chin. "Well, except for maybe your nick-name."

"But you're here to melt me?"

He flashed his teeth. "I'm trying."

It had been safer to pretend he was the help. Just the movie stuntman. Or the make-believe boyfriend. Not a man whose wealth dwarfed hers. One who had no use for her money or her fame and celebrity. One who'd put himself on the line to protect her—just because.

She didn't know what to do with a man like that. She'd spent years living as if she didn't need any man.

Because she could provide for herself, thanks. But with Rick, she was at a disadvantage. He'd come to her defense against a stalker, and now it turned out he was her boss. She didn't have the upper hand. He didn't need her for anything, either.

Well, except for sex. He clearly wanted her *badly*.

And what was wrong with making herself feel feminine and powerful for an interlude? After all, it wasn't as if she was giving up something. Except she risked falling for him.

The pent-up desire that she'd been feeling these weeks and refusing to acknowledge slipped from its shackles. Rick drove her crazy, and it was a thin line between being irritated and jumping his bones. Giving in meant easing some of the frustration, and suddenly nothing else mattered.

Seeming to read the assent in her eyes, Rick slowly took off her clothes, tossing the pieces aside one by one onto nearby furniture and peeling away her defenses to find what was in no way artifice. Then he shed some of his own clothes until they were both down to underwear.

She shivered as the cool air hit her.

"Let me warm you up," he muttered.

She wanted to say he already had, and that that was the problem. She was melting, her defenses flowing away like so much ice under a hot sun.

Chiara stepped out of the clothes pooled at her feet. Clad in just a lacy black bra and the barest slip of underwear, she had no mask. But if she felt nervous, the naked appreciation stamped on Rick's face put an end to it. She straightened her shoulders, and the resulting movement thrust her breasts forward, their peaks jutting against their thin covering.

Rick's face glowed with appreciation, and then he muttered what he wanted to do with her, his prominent arousal testimony to his words. Waves of heat washed over her, and she sucked in a breath.

He stepped forward, and when the backs of her legs hit the sofa, she let herself fall backward, bracing herself with one hand on a pillow. Rick followed, bent and took one of her nipples in his mouth through her bra, fabric and all, suckling her gently.

Chiara gasped, a strangled sound caught in her throat, and need shuddered through her. Her head fell back when he pushed aside her bra and transferred his attention to her other breast. She was awash in sensation, the universe popping with a kaleidoscope of color.

Rick knelt, pulled her to the end of the sofa arm so that her legs straddled it, and then pushed aside her underwear to use his mouth to love her some more. Cries of pleasure were ripped from her throat...and she felt herself splintering—until she bucked against him with her release.

Afterward, Rick straightened and shed his underwear like a man possessed. Watching him, Chiara stood up and did the same, her remaining garments melting away.

Rick suddenly cursed. "Damn it. Protection is still packed in my suitcase."

"I'm on contraception," she said throatily, dizzy with want.

His gaze caught with hers. "I want you to know I've gotten a clean bill from my doctor. I would never put you at risk."

She licked her lips. "Same goes for me."

They looked at each other for a moment, neither moving, savoring this moment.

And then Chiara held her hand out to him. "We're not going to make it to the bed, are we?"

He gave her a lopsided smile. "Stuntmen can do it everywhere."

Chiara followed his gaze to the nearby long leather ottoman, which doubled as a coffee table. *Oh.* As she bent to sit on it, Rick followed her down, giving her a long, sweet, lingering kiss.

When she embraced him, he entered her in one fluid movement, rocking her to her core. Joined to him, Chiara gave herself up to sensation, following the pace that Rick set.

When she felt Rick tighten, nearing his climax, she ran her hands over his ripped arms and bit back a moan.

"Let me hear you," Rick said as the air grew thick with their deep breathing.

"Rick, oh…now."

And just like that, as he thrust deep, Chiara felt herself coming apart again, dazed with her release.

Rick gave a hoarse shout and buried himself in her, collapsing into her embrace.

Chiara had never felt so at one with someone… exposed and yet secure.

As she walked by, Chiara glanced in her hallway mirror and resisted the urge to pinch herself. She looked happy…relaxed…and yes, sexually satisfied. Filming was over, so the main item on her agenda today was reading a script for a role that she was considering.

Ever since she and Rick had returned to LA from Welsdale two days ago, she'd been in a lovely cocoon. She flushed just thinking about what they'd done yesterday. Foreplay on the weight bench, but the exercise mat and even the jump rope had come in handy…

Walking into the den, she plopped herself on the couch, feet dangling off one end. She began reading the script on her tablet. Moments later, Rick walked in.

After an extraordinary bout of sex this morning, he'd gone out to run errands and she hadn't seen him in the two hours since. He looked just as yummy as earlier, however. They were both dressed in sweats, but somehow, he managed to make his look sexy rather than casual. He hadn't bothered shaving this morning, and she'd come to like the shadow darkening his jaw. Contrasting with his wonderful multihued eyes, it lent him an air of quiet magnetism…

Rick nodded toward the device in her hand. "Have you checked the news yet?"

"No, should I? I just sat down." She belatedly realized he looked more serious than usual.

Rick folded his arms and leaned against the entryway. "Well, the good news is your temporary restraining order came through, so your bad fan can be arrested for getting too close."

"Great." She hadn't given much thought to Todd Jeffers in the past several days, though now that she was back home and he knew her address, she supposed she did feel an undercurrent of more stress. She asked cautiously, "What's the bad news?"

"Your father has gotten himself arrested."

Chiara leaned her head back against the pillows and closed her eyes briefly. "In Sin City? What could he have possibly done? The police turn a blind eye to practically every vice imaginable there. Even prostitution is legal in parts of Nevada, for heaven's sake."

"Apparently he argued about a parking ticket."

"Sounds just like him. Responsibility has never been his strong suit."

"You have to deal with the daddy problem."

"I've never called him *Daddy*," she scoffed, straightening. "Sperm donor, maybe. Daddy, no."

"Whatever the name, you'll keep having the same pesky PR problems if you don't address the issue. And your next big movie might not come with a stuntman willing to double as the star's boyfriend."

"Hilarious." Still, she felt a pull on her heartstrings at the reminder that their arrangement was temporary and fake.

Rick dropped his arms and sauntered into the room. "We may have had some success in distracting the press from your father recently, but you need to turn around and face the issue."

"I don't run from anything," she scoffed again.

"Right. You're a daredevil. Guess who gave you the risk-taking gene?"

She shrugged off a sudden bad feeling as she got up. "I don't know what you're talking about."

Rick's gaze was penetrating. "What do you think gambling is? It's a high from taking risks. There's a rush from the brain's rewards system. You like risks, your father likes risks. Different species of risk, but same family."

She had *nothing* in common with her father. How dare Rick make that connection? Even worse, it was one she hadn't seen coming. So she was in a profession with big highs and lows... So she did some of her own stunts...

Rick folded his arms again. "The funny thing is the only situation where you won't take a chance is arranging a meeting with Michael Feran."

"I don't have anything to say to him."

Rick tossed her a disbelieving look. "Of course you do. You have a lifetime's worth of questions to grill and cross-examine him with," he said pleasantly, "but let's just stick with the issue at hand, which is getting him to stop attracting bad press."

She jutted her chin forward. "And how do you propose I do that?"

"I've got some ideas...ones that might appeal to his own self-interest."

"Oh? And since when have you turned into a psychologist?"

Rick braced his hands on his hips. "People management is part of the job description for a Hollywood producer. And stunt work is about getting your mind ready to conquer fear about what could happen to your body. Mind over body."

"Thanks for the tip."

"I also found your Las Vegas showgirl ventriloquist's dummy on the chair where you left her. She had plenty of insights about you," he joked, "but mostly she was content to just sit there and listen."

"She's trashy."

Rick choked on a laugh. "Great. She'll be popular."

"You like them that way," she accused.

"I like you. The dummy is just the repository for the part of your personality that you're afraid you might have inherited from your father."

"Oh, joy."

Rick suddenly sobered. "Your father has a gambling problem, and I understand addiction. Hal went back to drinking too much after Isabel's antics sent him into a spiral."

"You never mentioned there were consequences from Isabel's media stunt." She caught herself at Rick's droll look at the mention of the word *stunt*. "Sorry, bad choice of words. I meant her diva moment for the press."

Rick dropped his hands and shrugged. "Hal is sober these days after a stint in rehab. Or so I hear through the grapevine…since we don't socialize any-more."

Chiara was starting to understand more and more about Rick's wariness regarding the limelight, ac-tresses and fame in general. An aspiring actress had not only cost him a friendship but had crushed some-one he knew.

"I'll even offer my house for a meeting with your father," Rick went on. "Odele can contact Michael Feran and figure out the details, including flying him to Los Angeles. I'll pick up the tab."

She sighed before asking wryly, "So all I have to do is show up?"

"Affirmative."

"Your house isn't even finished!"

"There's landscaping and stuff still to be done, but it's habitable. And more important, it's neutral territory for a private meeting with your father." He raised his eyebrows.

"Is there anything you haven't thought of?" she demanded.

He gave her a lingering look. "There are still a few fantasies that I'm playing with…"

"You know, it's astonishing you come from such a nice family considering—"

"I'm an ego-driven macho stuntman who doesn't respect the rights of actresses to do their own dare-devil acts and knows nothing about the uses of double-sided tape?"

"No, considering your dirty mind."

One side of his mouth lifted in a smile. "Well,

that, too. I know plenty of uses for tape and blind-folds and silk ties."

Oh...wow.

Rick's eyes crinkled. "Stunts call for diverse props."

"I go propless."

Rick stepped closer and murmured, "Interesting. No need of any assistance?"

She tossed her hair back as sexual energy ema-nated off him in luscious waves that wrapped them-selves around her. "Yes, I go it alone."

He reached out and took a strand of her hair in his fingers. "Might be more fun if it's two."

"Or three or more?" she queried. "What's your limit? A menagerie?"

He gave a soft laugh. "A couple is good. The num-ber of times, on the other hand...limitless, I'd say."

Her breath started coming quick and shallow. *Oh.*

She swallowed and focused on the faint lines fan-ning out from the corners of his eyes, and the ones bracketing his mouth.

He lowered his head and then touched his lips to hers, and she sighed. He nudged her—once, twice, coaxing a response. *Open. Open.*

Chiara shivered and felt her breasts peak even though only their lips were touching. She leaned in, falling into something that she knew was bottom-less...still relatively unknown...and exciting.

Rick deepened the kiss and raked his fingers through her hair, his hand anchoring at the back of her head. They moved restlessly, unable to get enough of each other.

Then Chiara followed Rick's lead as they stripped off their clothes hurriedly, desperate for skin-on-skin contact. When they were down to underwear, he stopped her.

She drank him in from beneath lowered lashes. He was hot and male and vital. There was the ripped midriff, muscular arms, taut legs...the erection pushing against his boxers. Suddenly she needed to catch her breath.

He lowered the straps of her lacy bra and peeled the garment away from her, and then swallowed. "Chiara."

"Make love to me, Rick."

It was all the invitation that he needed. He kissed her with unrestrained passion, pulling her close as her arms wrapped around his neck. And she responded with a hunger of her own, the feel of his arousal against her fueling her passion.

When she broke away, she pushed down her panties and he did the same with his boxers. And then they were tumbling onto the sofa, reaching for each other in a tangle of limbs and desperate passion.

She grasped Rick's erection and began a pumping motion designed to stoke his passion and hers. He was warm, pulsating male—rigid with his need for her.

He tore her mouth from hers and expelled a breath. "Chiara, we've got to slow down or this is going to be over—"

"Before the director yells cut?" she purred. "There is no director, Stunt Stud."

He gave a strangled laugh. "Stunt Stud?"

"It's the name I came up with when I was objectifying you."

"I was going to say to slow down or this will be finished before you're satisfied."

"Worried I won't be able to keep up with you?" In response, she led his hand to her moist heat, already ready for him.

He stilled, and in the next moment, he was pushing her back against the pillows. Then he sheathed himself in one long stroke that had them both groaning.

As Rick hit her core, she arched her back, taking him in.

She followed his lead and the rhythm he set… building and building until she hit her climax in one husky cry.

"Chiara." In the moment after Rick called her name, he groaned, stiffened and then spilled inside her.

He slumped against her, and she cradled him.

Contentment rolled through her—a feeling that had been too elusive in her life until now…

Nine

When they pulled up in Rick's Range Rover to the nearly completed house, Chiara sucked in a breath. *Wow.*

Nervousness about the upcoming meeting with her father, who was scheduled to arrive within the hour, was replaced by happy surprise.

Rick's home wasn't a house but a castle. It was all gray stone and stunning turrets. She loved it.

She was so entranced that Rick had already come around and opened the car door for her before she thought to get out. She could see there was plenty of landscaping yet to be done, but still the effect from the outside was stunning.

"Want to take a look?" Rick teased as she got out.

"I'm sure you've seen plenty of impressive homes belonging to famous people."

None shaped like a castle. She looked at the mansion, and then glanced at Rick. "I'm impressed. You have the castle…were you looking for your fairy-tale princess?"

Rick's lips curved. "Only you can answer that, Snow."

He put his hand at her elbow. "Come on, let's look inside. It's done except for minor details, and is sparsely furnished."

Rick's house—*castle*—made her home look like a small and cute cottage.

Chiara gasped when they entered the foyer. She'd seen this house in her mind's eye.

The double-height entry was airy and sunny but also warm and inviting. Done in light colors, it belied the imposing exterior. A curving staircase led to the upper levels, and various open doorways offered glimpses of other parts of the house.

She followed Rick in a circuit of the ground floor. A warm, country-style kitchen with beige cabinetry and a large island connected to a spacious dining room. An immense living room was bifurcated by a two-way fireplace and was made cozy by coffered ceilings in a warm mahogany wood. A library, den, two bathrooms and a couple of storage rooms for staff rounded out most of the lower level. The only thing missing was furnishings for a family…

When they came full circle back to the entry, Chiara's gaze went to the staircase leading to the upper floors.

Rick adopted a teasing expression. "In case you are wondering, a home office with a built-in desk sits at the top of the principal turret. I haven't stashed a fairy-tale princess there."

"Rapunzel?" She tapped her chest. "Wrong fairy tale. I'm Snow, remember?"

Despite her joking, she felt comfortable here—too at home. It was almost enough to make her forget she was about to have one of the most significant meetings of her life.

She was an actress, she reminded herself sternly. She needed to adopt a persona—a shield—and get what she wanted out of this meeting.

As if reading her thoughts, Rick said, "You and your father can meet in the library. It has two club chairs and a coffee table at the moment."

"Okay." Why had she let Rick talk her into this? She knew he had a good point—dragons must be faced—but she wasn't relishing the chance to slay one of hers. She almost gave a nervous laugh at the thought of Rick cast as her knight in shining armor...

Except of course, she didn't believe in such knights or in Prince Charming—or in fairy tales, for that matter. Though she was having a hard time remembering that these days.

At the sound of a car pulling up, Rick said, "That must be him. I had a driver pick him up from the hotel where he stayed last night after his flight from Vegas."

"Oh, good," she managed, and then cleared her throat.

Rick looked at her searchingly, and then cupped her shoulders. "Are you okay?"

She gave him a blinding smile—one she usually reserved for the cameras. "Never better."

"Remember, you're in charge here. You hold the cards."

"Playing cards are what I intend to take out of his hands."

Rick lifted one side of his mouth. "Sorry, bad choice of words. I'll meet him outside and show him into the library."

"Of course." She'd dressed in a navy shirt dress—something she'd pulled out of the closet herself. Because even if Emery hadn't headed off to start her own fashion line, Chiara couldn't imagine asking a stylist about what to wear to a meeting with her estranged father. For some occasions in life, there was *no* fashion rule book.

Rick shoved his hands into his front pockets and nodded, the hair on his forearms revealed by rolled-up shirtsleeves. "Back soon."

When Rick turned away, Chiara walked into the library. And then, because she couldn't think of what else to do, she faced the partially open doorway… and waited.

The sound of quiet voices reached her. Greetings were exchanged…and then moments later, she heard footsteps.

Someone stepped into the library, and she immediately recognized Michael Feran—*her father.*

Her heart beat a thick, steady rhythm. She hadn't expected to feel this nervous. She hated that she did. *He* was the one who should be tense. After all, he'd walked out on her.

She hadn't seen him in person in years, but the media had made sure she hadn't forgotten what he looked like. She wished she could dismiss him as a gaunt and lonely gambling addict wallowing in his misery, but he looked…good.

She silently cursed the Feran genes. They'd graced her with the looks and figure that had propelled her to the top in Hollywood, but they also hadn't skipped a generation with Michael Feran. His salt-and-pepper hair made him look distinguished—a candidate for the father role in any big studio blockbuster.

"Chiara." He smiled. "It's wonderful to see you."

She wished she could say the same. Under the circumstances, it was a forced meeting.

At her continued silence, he went on, "I'm glad you wanted to meet with me."

"Rick convinced me that I needed to have this face-to-face meeting."

Michael Feran smiled. "Yes, how is the stuntman?" So her father read the press about her. *Of course.*

"I met him when I came in. Is he a candidate for future son-in-law?"

Chiara was hit with a sudden realization that left her breathless. She was falling for Rick. She had fallen for him. But they'd never discussed making their fake relationship permanent… She pushed aside the thought that had come with staggering clarity because if she dealt with any more emotion right now, she'd overload.

Instead, she forced herself to focus on Michael Feran. "You're creating unwanted publicity."

"I see."

"Why did you talk to that tabloid about me last year?" It was an unforgivable transgression to add to his list of sins.

"Money would be the easy answer."

She waited.

He heaved a sigh. "The hard one is that I wanted your attention."

"Well, you got it." She folded her arms.

She wasn't going to offer him a seat, and she sure wasn't going to sit down herself, despite the fact that Rick had pointed out this room had comfortable chairs. Michael Feran had to understand this was a halfhearted welcome and not an olive branch.

His gray brows drew together. "I probably didn't go about it in the best way. Believe it or not, it was the only time I took money from a reporter."

"Because you needed to pay off your gambling debts," she guessed.

He looked aggrieved. "It was a mistake. One I don't intend to make again."

She was definitely going to see to it that he didn't spill the beans again.

"Usually I'm winning at the card tables. Enough to pay my bills."

"Naturally. It's what matters in life." She couldn't help the tone of heavy sarcasm in her voice. "But you're generating bad press."

"Chiara—"

"Do you have any idea what it meant for a little girl to wake up wondering if her father had bolted again?" she interrupted, even while she didn't know why she was being so forthright. Maybe it was because, without even realizing it, she'd waited years for this opportunity to confront him about his misdeeds. Just as Rick had suggested.

"Chiara, I know I hurt you." Her father paused. "That's why I stopped showing up after you turned five. I thought that not making a sudden appearance was better than hurting you by coming and going."

He made it seem as if he'd done her a favor. She remembered the betting games they'd played when she was young. *I bet I can throw this pebble farther. Race you to the tree, loser is a rotten egg.* Even then Michael Feran hadn't been able to resist a bet. "You left a wife, a child, a home…"

"You don't know what it's like to walk away from a family—"

"I never would."

"—but you get to reinvent yourself with every film role."

"It's acting." First Rick, now her father. Was there no man in her life who could understand she was just pretending? She *liked* acting.

"You can become someone different, follow your dreams…"

Of course, but… She was so *not* going to feel sorry for him.

Michael sobered. "I can't turn back the clock."

She took a deep breath and addressed the elephant in the room. "Why did you leave that first time?"

She'd never asked because posing the question might be interpreted to mean she cared what the answer was. And she'd spent years making sure she didn't care—ignoring Michael Feran, leading her glamorous life and making sure her image stayed polished. Except he kept putting a dent in it.

Her father looked at her for a long moment, and then heaved another sigh. "I was an ambitious musician and I had dreams to follow, or so I thought."

She could relate to the career and the ambition part. Wasn't that what she'd spent her life pursuing? She loved acting…getting to know a character…and, yes, even getting immersed in a role. Except had she ever gotten to know herself—before Rick convinced her to stop and deal with her problems?

"I had some moderate success. We were the opening act for top singers. But I never broke through in the way you have." There was a note of pride in Michael Feran's voice, before he went on, "You're more successful than I was. Maybe…you always wanted to prove you could be more successful."

Again, she was floored by his observation. Had her drive to succeed been motivated by her need to outperform him—the absentee father? She'd never looked at it that way, but in any case she wasn't about to admit anything, so she said aloud, "You don't know me."

Michael Feran's face turned grave. "I don't. I don't know you, but I'd like to."

"As you said, we can't do a rewind."

"No, no, we can't." His face was grave, sad.

"You'd have to clean up your act if we're going to be any sort of family."

Where had that offer come from? But the minute the words were out of her mouth, her father perked up. *Her father.* Looking at his face, the resemblance was undeniable. She saw herself in the texture of his dark hair sprinkled with gray, in the shape of his face…in the slant of his aquiline nose.

Okay, she did feel sorry for him. He'd done very little for her since she was born, but he'd done even less for himself. Maybe it was for the best he hadn't been in her life. She'd been protected from the gambling…drifting… *Ugh.* It sounded just like life in Tinseltown, except she was committed to clean living even if she was based in Hollywood.

"I'd like to try," he said.

"Well, you're going to do more than try this time, you're going to succeed. You're checking into rehab for your gambling addiction." She felt…powerful…in control…*relieved.* She'd been the helpless kid who'd watched him walk away, not knowing when her father would be back, if ever. But this time, she was calling the shots.

She set down her terms. "I'm prepared to offer you a deal. You get into a facility to help with your problem and agree to stop making headlines. In return,

I'll cover your living expenses. The deal will be in writing, and you'll sign."

She had Rick to thank for that bit of inspiration. After their last sexual encounter, they'd sat in her garden and watched the sun set. He'd revealed himself to be more than a lover. He'd shown himself to be a partner and skilled negotiator who'd helped her come up with a plan for this meeting.

"And if I relapse?" There was a hint of vulnerability in her father's eyes that she hadn't expected.

"Then back to rehab you go…for as long as it takes."

He relaxed into a smile. "That's a gamble I'm willing to take."

"Because you have no choice."

"Because I want to improve if that means having a relationship with you, Chiara." As if he sensed she might argue, he continued in a rush, "It's too late for me to help raise you, but I hope we…can be family."

Family. Wasn't that what she'd yearned for when she'd been around the Serenghettis? And now here was her *father* offering the ties that bind. Choked up by emotion, she cleared her throat. "Fine, it's a role I'm willing to take on, but I'm putting you on notice, I expect an Oscar-worthy performance from you as a family member getting a second chance."

An unguarded look of hope crossed her father's face before he responded gruffly, "I have faith that the acting gene runs in the family."

* * *

Trouble for Chiara Feran and Her New Man? Sources Close to the Couple Admit That Blending Two Careers Is Causing Stress.

Chiara looked up from her cell phone screen and at Odele's expectant gaze. Her manager was clearly waiting to hear what Chiara thought about the web site that she'd told her to pull up.

They were sitting sipping coffee in the Novatus Studio commissary. Chiara had met Rick here earlier, where postproduction work had begun on *Pegasus Pride.* As an actress, she wasn't involved in picture and sound editing, but since Rick was a producer on this film, she'd tagged along when he'd said he was interested in checking in with Dan to see how things were going. Afterward, she'd made her way to the commissary to wait for Odele, so they could discuss business.

"Well, what do you think?" Odele asked in her raspy voice, nodding to the cell phone still clutched in Chiara's hand.

"You fed this story to *Gossipmonger*?"

Odele nodded. "I needed a way to hint at a possible end to your dalliance with Rick now that your father is going to rehab, while still keeping you in the public eye."

"I'm still wrapping my head around the fact that you didn't know Rick was a wealthy producer!"

Her manager shrugged. "He's a wily one, I'll admit. I thought I knew everyone in this town, but I guess I can be forgiven for not being acquainted with every silent investor in a film production company. Once you told me about the pile that he built in Beverly Hills, I realized I should have had him on my radar, though, I'll give you that."

"We don't need to rush to bring the ax down on the Chiara-Rick story, do we?" Chiara set down her phone, her heart heavy.

Odele was right. She no longer had to worry about her father making bad headlines, and she had Rick to thank for helping to engineer the resolution to that situation. It also meant she no longer *needed* Rick. Wasn't the entire purpose of their fake relationship to divert attention from her father's negative publicity?

Odele gave her a keen look. "No rush...but planning ahead wouldn't hurt, sweetie. Drop a few suggestions in the press that all might not be happily-ever-after. So when the story does end, it won't seem abrupt and it'll be a soft blow."

For whom? Chiara stifled the question even though she couldn't tell if Odele was referring to the hit to her or to her public image. Did it matter? The two were intertwined. She and Rick weren't a *relationship*, after all, but a *story*.

Chiara worried her bottom lip with her teeth. "Has Rick seen this headline?"

Odele adjusted her glasses. "Of course. I ran into him earlier when you'd momentarily left his side. He knows the script. He's known it from the beginning."

Chiara blanched and glanced down at her coffee cup. So he had seen it, and judging from Odele's expression, it hadn't ruffled him. He knew the bargain they'd struck.

Chiara squared her shoulders, seeing with clarity the road ahead—the path that had been there from the beginning. If she made the first move for a clean break, it didn't even have to damage Rick's reputation. She was familiar with how these things worked. A face-saving explanation would be issued. She could even see the headline: *Snow White and Prince Charming Go Their Separate Ways*.

She was doing Rick a favor. He'd never wanted to be tied to an actress…a *celebrity*. He could take his bow and retreat behind the curtain to his nice quiet life—on his large estate in LA. She was being fair.

But the two of them definitely needed to talk. *Soon. Right now.* Before she fell apart…or at least deeper into the warm cocoon of their relationship, where it was *her love* and his…*what*? He'd never come close to saying he loved her. Her heart squeezed and she blinked against a sudden swell of emotion.

She was a highly rated actress—she could do this.

She had sudden flashes from interludes in his arms. They'd been wonderful…but there'd been no promise of forever, and tomorrow started today. The next chapter.

Chiara looked at her watch. Rick was supposed to meet her here when he was done. And now she had more than enough to say to him…

She forced herself to continue her conversation with Odele, but twenty minutes later when her manager left to make her next meeting, Chiara was relieved…and then nervous as she waited for Rick to show up.

After a quarter of an hour, he walked in, looking casual…relaxed…happy. And as attractive as ever in gray pants and a white shirt.

Chiara swallowed when he gave her a quick peck on the lips.

He sat down across from her at the small table and then lounged back in his chair.

"How did your meeting with Dan end?" she asked brightly.

"Fine. The editor showed up and we discussed plans for the rough cut." He cracked a grin. "Dan's grateful to you for not needing many retakes and keeping us on schedule. Everything's looking great, and with any luck, the box office receipts will reflect it."

They talked about the postproduction work for a few more minutes. Then when the conversation reached a lull, she jumped in and said, "So you must be relieved." He looked at her quizzically, and she shrugged. "Odele's latest planted story in the press."

"I don't give a damn about Odele's PR moves."

His words surprised her, but then hadn't he always been anti-publicity?

"Okay, but we need to talk—" she wet her lips "—because the reason we got together as a couple no longer exists."

She willed him to…what? Get down on bended knee and pledge his eternal love? She'd said all along that she didn't believe in fairy tales.

She smiled tentatively. "Thank you for helping me resolve the impasse with my father. He loves your idea of the two of us partnering to combat his gambling addiction." Her expression turned wry. "Odele likes it, too, of course. She thinks it would be a good way to turn a negative story into a positive one. I could even take it on as a charitable cause."

Rick inclined his head but looked guarded. "Okay, yeah."

"But now that the problem with my father is gone," she said, taking a deep breath, "we no longer have to continue this farce."

Had she really said *farce*? She'd meant to say...

Rick's expression hardened. "Right."

"You disagree?"

He leaned in. "You're still that little girl who is afraid of being abandoned—of someone walking out on her again."

"Please, I know where you're going with this is, and it's not true." It wasn't abandonment she was scared of. She was a grown woman who feared she'd have her heart broken. *Her heart was broken*—because she was in love with Rick and he steered clear of actresses.

Still, wasn't his keen perception what she liked about him? Loved? Yes, *loved*—in addition to his humor, intelligence and daring. They were qualities that appealed to different sides of her personality, even if they made her uncomfortable and yes, infuriated her sometimes.

"What about your overeager admirer?" Rick demanded.

"That's my problem to deal with."

"And mine."

She furrowed her brow. "What do you mean?"

"I mean my role here wasn't solely to play boyfriend but to make sure you stayed safe."

Her eyes narrowed. "Odele hired you?"

"She didn't need to hire me. Do you know how much money I have invested in *Pegasus Pride*? Keeping the main talent safe was inducement enough."

She felt his words like a blow to the chest. All those lingering touches, kisses, and his motivation had been... "You lied to me."

"Not really. You knew I was primarily a fake boyfriend."

"And secondarily a rat."

He raised his eyebrows. "You're offended because I may have had ulterior motives, too, in this game of ours?"

Yes, it had been a game. She was the fool for forgetting that. "I'm annoyed for not being told the whole truth. At least I was clear about my motivations."

"Yes, and you're determined not to rely on any man, aren't you?"

"Was Odele in on this?" she countered.

He shrugged. "We might have had a conversation about how it was in everyone's interest for me to keep an eye on you."

"Everyone's interest but mine," she said bitterly.

Rick set his jaw. "It was in your best interest, too, though you're too pigheaded to admit it."

Her heart constricted. Had he meant those things he'd whispered in the heat of passion—or had she run into the biggest actor of all? Even now, the urge to touch him was almost irresistible.

How had this conversation gotten very serious and very bad so fast? She'd wanted to talk about their charade and give him an out that she hoped he *wouldn't* take. Instead, she was left deflated and wondering whether she'd ever understood him.

Still, she rallied and lifted her chin. "You should be glad I'm setting you free. We never talked about forever, and you don't like fame. You don't want to be dating an actress, even if it's pretend." Two could play at this game. If he was going to cast her as another high-maintenance starlet, albeit one with an aversion to vulnerability where men were concerned, then she could portray him as camera-shy and hung up on celebrity.

He firmed his jaw but took a while to answer. "You're right. Fame isn't my thing." He raked a hand through his hair. "I should have learned that lesson with Isabel."

Chiara held back a wince. In some ways, she understood. The last thing some stars' egos could handle was to be cast in someone else's shade. There were A-list celebrities who refused to date other A-list celebrities for that very reason. Still, it rankled. She was not some random fame-seeker. If she couldn't fall in love with a celebrity, and an anonymous civil-

ian would be put off her fame, who was left? Did she
have to settle for a brief interlude with a stuntman
with hidden layers? Was that all there was for her?

She lifted her chin, willing it to hold firm. "It's
probably best if you moved out at this point. We could
do with some space." Then she decided to echo Odele.
"It'll plant the seeds for when our breakup is announced."

Rick's expression tightened. "Can't forget to spin
it for the press, right?"

Ten

Chiara looked in her bathroom mirror. It had been a month since her breakup with Rick. A sad, depressing but uneventful month...*until now*.

She looked down at the stick in her hand. There was no mistaking the two telltale lines. Two lines that were about to change her life. She was pregnant.

The irony wasn't lost on her. She'd been wrestling with how to combine a career with her desire to start a family. Now the decision had been made for her.

As she disposed of the stick in the bathroom's wastepaper basket, she thought back to the last time she and Rick had been intimate—and her mind whirled.

She'd recently discovered that she'd expelled her contraceptive ring. It had probably gotten dislodged during rigorous sex, and then gone down the toilet afterward without her knowing it. Preoccupied with her breakup with Rick, she hadn't dwelled too much on it. But now...

Chiara looked at herself in the bathroom mirror as she washed her hands. She didn't look any different—*yet*.

She'd spent years trying not to be pregnant. She had a career to tend.

But while it wasn't the best of circumstances, it wasn't the worst, either. *A baby.* She was in her early thirties, financially independent, and had an established career. She'd always wanted a child, and in fact had started worrying that she couldn't see how it was going to happen. It had finally come to pass, but in a way she hadn't planned or foreseen. She'd been drawn to the Serenghettis, and now she was pregnant with an addition to the family. If things had been different—if Rick had loved her—she'd have been overjoyed right now instead of shadowed with worry. Still, she let giddiness seep through her. *A baby.*

She walked into her bedroom and sat on the bed, taking a calming breath. Then she picked up the phone receiver, toyed with it and replaced it. She had to tell Rick, of course...but she just needed time to process the information herself first. This wasn't avoidance or procrastination. At least that's what she kept telling herself...

She got up, paced, went downstairs to poke around in her fridge and then came upstairs again to stare at her phone.

When she couldn't stand it any longer, she called Odele and spilled all to her manager.

Odele was surprisingly equanimous at the news.

"Don't you know this means I'll be too pregnant to take on another action movie?" Chiara demanded, because she knew career suicide was at the top of Odele's list of sins.

"You wanted to stop doing them anyway."

Chiara lowered her shoulders. "Yes, you're right."

"What was Rick's reaction?"

"I haven't told him yet. I've been working up to that part."

There was a long pause on the line as Odele processed this information. "Well, good luck, honey. And remember, it's best to eat the frog."

"We fairy-tale types are supposed to kiss them, not eat them," Chiara joked weakly. "But okay, I get your point about doing the hard stuff first and getting it over with."

"Exactly."

"I just…" She took a deep breath. "I'm not sure I'm prepared to make that call to Rick." *Just yet.*

"I'm always here to help."

"Thanks, Odele."

The next day, Chiara wasn't feeling calm exactly, but she'd come down from her crazy tumult of emotions. She ventured out to her doctor's office for a consultation, having gotten herself an early appointment after there was a cancellation.

She didn't go into detail with the staff on the phone. She knew how juicy a piece of gossip a pregnant actress was, and medical staff had been known for leaks despite confidentiality laws. Out of an abundance of caution, she wore sunglasses and a scarf when she showed up for her appointment—because the paparazzi also knew that staking out the offices of doctors to the stars was a great way to get a scoop, or at least a tantalizing photo.

Dr. Phyllia Tribbling confirmed she was pregnant and assured her that everything was fine. She told her to come back when she was a few weeks further along.

Chiara found she was calmer after the doctor's visit, no doubt due to the obstetrician's soothing manner.

She spent the rest of the day researching pregnancy online. She didn't dare visit a bookstore—and certainly not a baby store—because of the risk of being spotted by the press. Instead, she stayed home and took a nap. She should have read the signs in her unusual weariness lately, but pregnancy had been the last thing on her mind.

When she woke late in the day, she checked herself for any sign of morning sickness, but didn't feel a twinge. With the all-clear, she fixed herself a salad and a glass of water. Walking into the den, she sat on the sofa and placed the food on a coffee table.

After a few bites, she scrolled through the day's news on her phone.

When she came across a headline about herself, it took her a moment to process it, but then she nearly collapsed against the cushions.

Chiara Feran Is Pregnant!

She scanned the article and reread it, and then with shaking fingers, called her manager.

"Odele," she gasped. "How did *Gossipmonger* get this info?"

"They probably saw you exiting the doctor's office, sweetie," Odele said calmly. "You know, paparazzi like to stalk the offices of celebrity gynecologists and obstetricians."

"I just got back! Not even the gossip sites operate that fast." Chiara shook her head, even though her manager wasn't there to see it. "I should have worn a wig."

"I don't think that would have done the trick," Odele said drily. "Now, not getting knocked up to begin with, that would have done it."

Chiara's eyes narrowed. "You didn't feed them this story, did you?"

"No."

"But did you slip someone a tip to watch the doctor's office?" Chiara pressed.

"You have a suspicious mind."

"Did you?"

"I might have mentioned Dr. Tribbling has seen a lot of business lately."

"Odele, how could you!"

"Why don't you call Mr. Stuntman and let him know he isn't shooting blanks?" Odele answered sweetly.

"Why?" Chiara was close to wailing. She'd done it

enough times on-screen to know when she was nearing the top of the emotional roller coaster.

"Better to squelch the rumor fast that you've broken up with Rick. Otherwise we'll be putting out fires for months. The press loves a story about a spurned pregnant woman going it alone."

Chiara took a breath. "Rick and I are broken up. Period."

"Not as far as the press is concerned. They're going to love stringing your two names together in real and virtual ink."

"And that's the only thing that matters, right?"

"No...it isn't." Odele sighed, softening. "Why don't you talk to him? Then reality and public perception can be aligned."

Chiara steeled herself and took a deep gulping breath. "Odele, you're fired."

They were words she'd never thought she'd say, but she'd had enough of manipulation...of public scrutiny...of Hollywood...and yes, of one stuntman in particular.

"Sweetie, you're overwrought, and it can't be good for the baby. Take time to think about it."

"Goodbye, Odele."

Yes, she'd calm down...right after she burst into tears.

Rick spit out his morning coffee. The hot liquid hit the oatmeal bowl like so many chocolate chips dotting cookie batter.

He prided himself on being unflappable. A cool

head and calm nerves were a must in stunt work, particularly when something unexpected happened. But as with everything concerning Chiara, levelheadedness walked out the door with his better judgment.

He looked around his West Hollywood rental, still his home since Chiara had canceled his roommate privileges and his Beverly Hills place wasn't finished. The rain hitting the windows suited his mood. Or rather, it fit the rest of his life, which stretched out in a dull gray line in front of him. He got the same adrenaline rush from being with Chiara as he did from stunts, which probably explained the colorlessness of his days since their breakup.

Except now… *Chiara was pregnant.*

Rick was seized by turns with elation and shock. A baby. His and Chiara's. He was going to be a father.

Of course he wanted kids. He'd just never given much thought to how it would happen. He was thirty-three and at some point he'd be too old for stunt work. Sometime between now and then, his life would transition to something different. He figured he'd meet a woman, get married and have kids. Except along the way, he'd never foreseen a fake relationship with a maddening starlet who would then turn up pregnant.

Suddenly someday was now…and it wasn't supposed to happen this way—knocking up an actress tethered to fame when they weren't even married, living together or talking about forever.

Chiara infuriated and amused him by turns, the combustible passion between them feeding on itself. They were good together. Hell, he'd thought things had been heading to…something. But never mind. She'd made it clear he'd served his purpose and now there was no role for him in her life.

Now, though, whether she liked it or not, he had a place. She was pregnant.

He wondered whether this announcement was a public relations ploy, and then dismissed the idea. Chiara had too much integrity. He knew that much even though they were no longer a couple.

Still, she hadn't had the decency to tell him, and his family would be reading the news online and in print, just like everyone else. Her handlers hadn't yet sent out a second volley in this juicy story, but already he was looking like a jerk. *He just broke up with her, and now his ex-girlfriend has announced she's pregnant.* That's what everyone would think. *Maybe he left her because there was a surprise baby.*

There was one thing to do—and he wasn't waiting for an invitation. He still had the passcode to Chiara's front gate, unless she'd changed it.

Rick got his wallet, keys and phone, and then made a line for the door. He'd woken up this morning moody and out of sorts—more or less par for the course for him since his breakup with Chiara, but that was even before realizing he'd been served up as delicious gossipy dish for his neighbors to consume along with their morning coffee.

He cursed. "Moody" had just given way to "flaming-hot pissed off."

He made record time on the way to Chiara's house, adrenaline pumping in his veins. He knew from experience working on stunts that he was operating on a full head of steam. He needed to force himself to take a breath, slow down, collect his thoughts... *Hell.*

A baby. And she hadn't told him.

When he got to Chiara's front gate, rationality returned enough for him to pause a moment and call her from his cell. The last thing he needed was for Chiara to assume her surprise visitor was her stalker.

"It's Rick, and I'm coming in," he announced when she picked up, and then hit the end button without waiting for a response.

When he got to the house, the front door was unlocked and he let himself in.

He found Chiara in the kitchen, dressed in an oversize sweater and leggings, a mug in one hand.

His gaze went to her midriff, before traveling back to her face. Not that she would be showing yet—but she did look weary, as if she hadn't slept well. He resisted the urge to stride over and wrap her in his arms.

"I assume you unlocked the door for me when I called from the gate and that you don't have a standing invitation for your overeager fan to walk in." It was a mild reproach, much less than he wanted to say.

She set the mug down. "What do you think?"

"You're *pregnant.*" The last word reverberated through the room like the sound of a brass bell.

Chiara blanched.

"I found out the news with the rest of the world."

"I didn't have time to call you first." She wrung her hands. "The story broke so fast."

"You could have called me when the pregnancy test came back positive."

She hugged her midriff with her arms. "I wanted to be sure. I only went to the doctor yesterday."

"How did this happen?" he asked bluntly.

She raised her eyebrows. "I think you know."

"Right." *Mind-blowing sex.*

"My contraceptive ring accidentally fell out, and I didn't notice. I didn't give it much thought when I realized what happened." She shrugged. "I've always wanted kids. I guess it's happening sooner than I anticipated."

A very real sense of relief washed over him at her words. She wanted this baby, but birth control failure had led to very real consequences for the both of them. "You're going to announce we're still together."

She blinked. "Why?"

"Why? Because I don't want to look like a first-class jerk in front of the world, that's why."

"That your reason?" She appeared bewildered and a flash of hurt crossed her face.

"Aren't you the one who has been all about public image until now?" he tossed back. "Maybe this pregnancy is another PR stunt."

She dropped her arms, her expression turning shocked and offended. *"What?"*

"Are you saying Odele didn't plant the story in *Gossipmonger*?"

"I didn't know anything about it!"

He let another wave of satisfaction wash over him before he turned all-business. "Anyway, it doesn't matter. We're going to start acting and pretending like we never have before—the happy couple expecting a bundle of joy."

She lifted her chin. "I don't need your help."

He knew Chiara had the resources, but that was beside the point. "Sweetheart," he drawled, making the endearment sound ironic, "whether you want it or not, you've got it."

"Or?"

"Odele will be needing medication to deal with the ugly media firestorm."

"And will a wedding in Vegas follow?" she asked sarcastically. "I'll need to put Odele on retainer again."

"Whatever works."

She threw up her hands. "It's ridiculous. How long do you plan for this to go on?"

Until he figured out his next steps. He was buying himself time. "Until I don't look like a loser who abandoned his girlfriend the minute she turned up pregnant."

Rick paced in the nearly empty library of his multimillion-dollar new home. Raking his fingers through his hair, he stared out the French doors at the blazing sunshine bathing his new property in light. He'd just met with a landscaper and walked over the grounds. This morning, his appointment had been uppermost in his mind...until he'd checked the news.

Still, what was it all for? He'd bought and renovated this house as a keen investor...but now it felt insignificant. Because what really mattered in his life was half a city away. *Pregnant. With his baby.*

His gaze settled on the two upholstered armchairs. He'd brokered a cease-fire and even a rapprochement between Chiara and her father, but he couldn't figure out how to dig himself out of a hole—except by muscling in on Chiara earlier and ordering her to get back together until he figured things out. But then what?

His cell phone buzzed, and he fished it out of his pocket.

"Rick." Camilla Serenghetti's voice sounded loud and clear.

Rick hadn't even bothered to look at who was calling. He hadn't had a chance to figure out what to say to his family, but it was showtime.

"I read I'm going to be a grandma, but I know it can't be true. My son would have told me such happy news."

Of course.

"I told Paula at the hairdresser, 'No, no, don't listen to *Gossipmonger*. I know the truth.'" Pause. "Right?"

Rick raked a hand through his hair. "I just found out myself, Mom."

His mother muttered something in Italian. "So it is true? *Congratulazioni*. I can't believe it. First Cole has a surprise wedding. Now you have a surprise baby."

"You still have Jordan and Mia to count on." His remaining siblings might go a more traditional route.

"No, no. I'm happy...*happy* about the baby." His mother sounded emotional. "But no more surprises. *Basta*—enough, okay?"

"I'd like nothing better," he muttered, because he'd gotten the shock of his life today.

When he got off the phone, he texted his siblings.

The gossip is true, hang tight.

He knew he had to deal with stamping out questions—or at least holding them off—until he figured things out. Before he could put away his cell, though, his phone rang again.

"Rick."

"What can I do for you?" Rick recognized the voice, and under the circumstances, Chiara's father was the last person he wanted to have a conversation with. Michael Feran had his number from when he'd helped broker the meeting with Chiara, but he'd never expected the older man to use it.

"This is an odd request."

"Spit it out." The words came out more harshly than Rick intended, but it had already been a hell of a day.

Michael Feran cleared his throat. "I can't get in touch with Chiara."

Great. "What did you do, Michael?"

"Nothing. I called her at eleven, when we'd agreed to talk."

Rick knew Chiara had opted to periodically touch base with her father now that she was paying his bills.

"No one answered."

"I was heading out, and I'm not far from her house. I'll swing by." He didn't examine his motives. Michael Feran had given him another excuse to see Chiara, and maybe this time they could have a more satisfactory meeting—one that didn't end with her turning away and him walking out.

Besides, she was pregnant. His gut tightened. She could really be in trouble.

"Good." An edge of relief sounded in the older man's voice. "And I understand congratulations are in order."

"To you, too."

"Thank you. I just got an invite to be a father again. I didn't expect being a *grandfather* to be part of the bargain. At least not so soon."

"I'm sure," Rick replied curtly. "But one thing at a time. I'll go check on the mother-to-be now."

After ending the call, Rick made for the front door. For the second time that day, he found himself racing to Chiara's house, adrenaline thrumming through his veins.

She was fine. She had to be fine. She was probably dealing with pregnancy symptoms and in no mood to talk to her father. In the meantime, he might have another opportunity to set things to rights between them.

Marry me. The words popped into his head without thought, but of course they were the right ones. Right, natural…logical.

Exiting his house, he got behind the wheel of his Range Rover for the drive to Brentwood. Fortunately, traffic was light, and he reached Chiara's house faster than he expected.

When he reached her front gate, he tried calling her again. And when she didn't answer, he stabbed in the security code, jaw tightening.

Moments later, he pulled up in front of Chiara's house and saw her car parked there. His gut clenched. *Why isn't she answering her phone?*

Noticing the patio door open at the side of the house, he strode toward it…and then froze for a second when he realized there was broken glass on the ground.

Stepping inside the house, he could sense someone was there. Then he saw a man reflected in a mirror down the hall. The intruder crouched and ducked into the next room.

Rick's blood pumped as he raced forward. Damn it, he'd be lucky if this was an ordinary street burglar. But the brief glimpse he'd caught said this guy resembled Chiara's stalker.

Chiara came out of the marble bath in her bedroom suite and then walked into the dressing room. She pulled underwear and exercise clothes from a dresser and slipped into them.

In order to help her relax, she'd just taken a shower—and intended to take another after her workout. Her doctor had cleared her for moderate exercise in her first trimester.

After her argument with Rick earlier, she'd been torn between wanting to cry and to wail in frustration. Her life had been a series of detours and blind turns lately…

She went downstairs to her home gym, and then glanced out the window at the overcast day. It suited her mood. Even the weather seemed ready to shed some tears…

Suddenly she spotted a hunched figure darting across the lawn. Frowning, she moved closer to the window. She wasn't expecting anyone. She had a regular cleaning service, and a landscaper who came once a week, but she didn't employ a live-in caretaker. There was no reason to, since she was often away on a movie set herself. Still, thanks to her fame, and now a sometime stalker, she had high fences, video cameras, an alarm system and a front gate with a security code. Even if she no longer had a bodyguard…

How had he gotten in?

As Chiara watched, the intruder slipped around the side of the house and out of view. Moments later, she heard a crash and froze. She ran over to the exercise room door and locked it.

Spinning around, she realized how vulnerable she was. Her workout clothes didn't have pockets, and she'd left her cell phone upstairs. She'd also never put a landline extension in this room, because there'd seemingly been no need to. The gym was on the first floor and faced a steep embankment outside. While it would be hard for someone to get in, it also meant she was trapped.

She heard the distant noise of someone moving around in the house. Her best bet was to stay quiet. She hoped whoever it was wouldn't look in here—

at least not immediately. In the meantime, she had to figure out what to do… If the intruder wandered upstairs, perhaps she could make a dash for freedom and quietly call 911.

She heard the sound of a car on the gravel drive and almost sobbed with relief. Whoever it was must have known the security code at the front gate. Her heart jumped to her throat. *Rick?*

He didn't know about the intruder. He could be hurt, or worse, killed. She had to warn him.

Only a minute later, voices—angry and male— sounded in the house, but the confrontation was too indistinct for her to make out what was said.

"Chiara, if you're here, don't move!" Rick's voice came to her from the rear of the house.

She heard a scuffle. Something crashed as the combatants seemed to be fighting their way across the first floor.

Ignoring Rick's order, she wrenched open the door to the exercise room and dashed out in the direction of the noise. The sight that confronted her in the den made her heart leap to her throat all over again. Rick was pummeling Todd Jeffers, and while Rick appeared to have the upper hand, his opponent wasn't giving up the fight.

She looked around for a way to help and found herself reaching for a small marble sculpture that her interior decorator had positioned on a side table.

Grabbing it, she approached the two men. As her stalker staggered and then righted himself, she brought the sculpture down on the back of his head with a resounding thud.

Jeffers staggered again and fell to his knees, and Rick landed a knee jab under his chin. Her stalker sprawled backward, and then lay motionless.

Rick finally looked up at her. He was breathing heavily, and there was fire in his eyes. "Damn it, Chiara, I told you not to come out!"

As scared as she was, she had her own temper to deal with. "You're welcome." Then she looked at the figure at their feet. "Sweet heaven, did I kill him?"

"Heaven is unlikely the place he'll be," Rick snarled.

"So I killed him?" she squeaked.

Rick bent to examine Jeffers and then shook his head. "No, but he's passed out cold."

She leaped for the phone even though what she wanted to do was throw up from sudden nausea. "I have to call 911."

"Do you have any rope or something else we can tie him up with?" Rick asked. "He's unconscious but we don't know for how long."

With shaky fingers, she handed him the receiver. While Rick called the police, she ran to get some twine she kept for wrapping presents. Her uninvited guest needed to be hog-tied, not decorated with a pretty bow, but it was all she had.

As she passed through the house, she noticed some picture frames had been repositioned—as if her stalker had stopped to admire them—and some of her clothes had been moved. Chiara shuddered.

Likely Jeffers's obsession with her stuff had bought her time—time enough to stay hidden in the gym until Rick arrived.

Eleven

Chiara sat in her den attempting to get her bearings. Todd Jeffers was on his way to prison, not least because he'd violated a restraining order by scaling her fence, taking advantage of the fact that her alarm system had been off and she'd been ignoring the video cameras. Breaking and entering, trespassing... Thanks to Rick, the police would throw the book at him.

While Rick walked the remaining police to the door, she called Odele. She needed someone who would deal with the inevitable press attention. And even though she'd uttered the words *you're fired*, she and Odele were like family—and there was nothing like a brush with danger and violence to mend fences. She filled in her manager on what had happened, and

Odele announced she would drive right over—both to get the fuller story, and perhaps because she sensed Chiara needed a shoulder to lean on.

Because Rick wasn't offering one—he continued to look mad as hell.

She knew she was lucky Rick had shown up at the right moment. She'd been in the shower when her father had attempted to reach her, and because he was worried she hadn't picked up, he'd called Rick. Michael Feran had done nothing for her...until today, when he may have saved her life. The ground beneath her had shifted, and there hadn't even been a major seismological event in LA. Forgetting about her scheduled call with her father had been a lucky break because minutes later she'd had an intruder in her house.

When Rick walked back in, Chiara hugged her arms tight across her chest as she sat on her couch.

He looked like a man on a short leash. The expression on his face was one she'd never seen before—not even in the middle of a difficult stunt. He was furious, and she wondered how much of it was directed at her.

"Thanks," she managed in a small voice.

"Damn it, Chiara!" Rick ran his hand through his hair. "What the hell? I told you to get extra security."

"You were it. I didn't have time to replace you... yet."

"You didn't have time? There's been a court order in place for weeks!"

She stood up. "Sarcastic stuntmen willing to

moonlight as bodyguard and pretend boyfriend are hard to come by."

"Well, you almost gained an unwelcome husband!" Rick braced his hands at his sides. "According to the police, your Romeo had picked a wedding date and drafted a marriage announcement before he showed up today."

Chiara felt the hairs on the back of her neck rise. As a celebrity, she'd gotten some overzealous adulation in the past, but this was beyond creepy. "Don't lecture me."

She was frustrated, overwhelmed and tired— nearly shaking with shock and fear. She needed comfort but Rick was scolding her. It was all too much.

Rick crouched beside her. "We need to resolve this."

She raised her chin. "My stalker is behind bars. So that's another reason I don't need you anymore, I guess."

Except she did. She loved him. But he'd offered nothing in return, and she couldn't stay in a relationship based on an illusion. She'd learned this much from Tinseltown: she didn't want make-believe. She didn't want a relationship made for the press, and the false image of a happy couple expecting their first child. She wanted true love.

Rick stood up, a closed look on his face. He thrust his hands in his pockets. "Right, you don't need me. You'll never need any man. Got it. Your father may be back in your life, but you always stand on your own."

She said nothing. In her mind, though, she willed

him to give her the speech that she really wanted. *I love you. I can't live without you. I need you.*

He braced his hands on his sides. "We're stuck playing out this drama, the two of us. The press junket for *Pegasus Pride* is coming up, and we don't want to be the story instead of the movie. I'll move back in with you here until my house is ready. We'll do promo for the movie and then nest until the baby arrives. All the while, we're back to Chiara and Rick, the happy expectant couple, as far as the press is concerned."

She lifted her chin again. "Got it."

The only thing that saved her from saying more was Odele breezing in the front door and descending like a mother hen.

"Oh, honey," her manager exclaimed.

Chiara looked at her miserably and then eyed Rick. "I'm glad you're here because Rick was just leaving to pack. He's moving back in with me."

"I'll be back soon."

She'd dreamed about their getting back together, but it wasn't supposed to happen like this.

Rick looked around his West Hollywood rental, debating what to pack next. The movers could do the rest.

Chiara's stalker may have been arrested, but the threat to Rick's own sanity remained very real. He'd always prided himself on being Mr. Cool and Unflappable—with nerves of steel in the face of every stunt. But there was nothing cool about his relationship with Chiara.

"So the first Serenghetti grandbaby, and it was a surprise." Jordan shook his head as he taped a box together. "Mom must be beside herself."

His brother happened to be in town for another personal appearance, so he'd come over to help Rick pack. Together, they were surrounded by boxes in the small living room.

"Last I heard, she was trying three new recipes." Rick knew cooking was stress relief for his mother.

Damn it, he wished the news had broken another way. Yet, if Chiara was to be believed, it wasn't her doing that the cat was out of the bag.

Jordan shook his head. "Of course Mom is cooking. First Cole throws an unexpected wedding, now you hit her with a surprise grandchild. She's probably trying to figure out what went wrong with her parenting recipe—was she missing an ingredient?'

"Hilarious," Rick remarked drily. "She's got two more kids she can hang her hopes on."

Jordan held up his hands as if warding off a bad omen. "You mean, she has Mia to help her out."

Rick shrugged. "Whatever."

His brother looked around. "You know we could just throw this stuff in a van ourselves instead of using movers."

"Yeah, but I've got more pressing problems at the moment."

Jordan cocked his head. "Oh, yeah, daddy duty. But that doesn't start for another…?"

"Seven months or more," Rick replied shortly.

Chiara had gotten pregnant in Welsdale or soon

after. There'd been plenty of opportunities. Once the floodgates had opened, they hadn't been able to keep their hands off each other.

"You know, I was debating what housewarming gift to get you. Now I'm thinking you need one of those dolls they use in parenting classes…to practice diapering and stuff."

"Thanks for the vote of confidence."

"Well, you and Chiara are definitely in the express lane of relationships," Jordan remarked.

"The relationship was a media and publicity stunt."

Jordan's face registered his surprise. "Wow, the work of a stuntman never ends. I'm impressed by your range."

"Put a lid on it, Jordan."

His brother flashed a grin. "Still, a publicity stunt…but Chiara winds up pregnant? How do you explain that one?"

"I was also supposed to protect her from her stalker friend. That was the real part."

Jordan picked up his beer and toasted him with it. "Well, you did do that. I suppose one thing led to another?"

"Yeah, but it could have gone better." The nut job had already been in Chiara's house when he'd arrived. As for the relationship part…

"Or worse."

Rick's hand curled at his side. Damn it. Why hadn't Chiara listened to him and taken more precautions? Because she was hardheaded.

Jordan shook his head. "I can't believe I had to get the news from *Gossipmonger.*"

"Believe it. Chiara's team has a contact there."

"Still, I figured I'd hear it from you. I thought the brotherly bond counted for something," Jordan said in a bemused tone.

"You didn't need to know it was a publicity stunt."

His brother shrugged. "It seemed real enough to me. So what are you going to do?"

"For the moment, I'm moving back in with her. What does it look like I'm doing?"

Jordan nodded, his expression blank. "So you're muscling back into her life. Do you know an approach besides caveman-style?"

"Since when are you a relationship expert?"

"This calls for a grand gesture."

Rick nearly snorted. "She's practically announced she doesn't need a knight on a horse."

Jordan shrugged. "She doesn't need you, you don't need her, but you want each other. Maybe that's what you have to show her." His brother's lips quirked. "You know, upend the fairy tale. Show up on a horse and tell her that she needs to save you."

Rick frowned. "From what?"

Jordan grinned. "Yourself. You've been bad-tempered and cranky."

"So says the Serenghetti family philosopher who only does shallow relationships."

Jordan placed his hand over his heart. "My guru powers only work with others."

Rick threw a towel at his brother, who caught it deftly. "Get packing."

Still, he had to admit Jordan had given him some ideas.

"You look like a miserable pregnant lady," Odele remarked.

"My best role yet." Chiara felt like a mess...or rather, her life was one. Ironically the situation with her father was the only part she'd straightened out.

After yesterday's drama, Odele had stayed over, feeling Chiara needed someone in the house with her. And Chiara was thankful for the support. She'd let herself cry just once...

Chiara toyed with her lunch of salmon and fresh fruit. Outside the breakfast nook, the sun shone bright, so unlike yesterday. Her mood should have picked up, too, but instead she'd been worried about spending the next months with Rick in her house—falling apart with need, so unlike her independent self.

"I hate to see you make a mistake," Odele remarked from across the table.

Was that regret in her manager's voice? "You sound wistful."

"I'm speaking from experience. There was one who got away. Don't let that be your situation."

"Oh, Odele."

"Don't *Odele* me," her manager said in her raspy voice. "These days there's a fifty-three-year-old editor at one of those supermarket rags who is just waiting for a date with yours truly."

Chiara managed a small laugh. "Now, that's more like it."

Odele's eyes gleamed. "He's too young for me."

"At fiftysomething? It's about time someone snatched him out of the cradle."

"I'll think about it…but this conversation isn't about me, honey. It's about you."

Chiara sighed. "So how am I supposed to avoid making a mistake? Or are you going to tell me?"

"I've got an idea. You and Rick are meant to be together. I've thought so for a long time." She shook her head. "That's why—"

"This pregnancy is a sign from the heavens?"

"No, your moping expression is."

Chiara set down her fork. "I guess I'm not as good an actress as I thought."

"You're a great actress, and I've lined up Melody Banyon at *WE Magazine*. She can come here for an interview tomorrow." Her manager harrumphed. "My second attempt at making you and Rick see reason."

"Another of your schemes, Odele?" she said, and then joked, "Haven't we had enough of the press?"

"Trust me, you're going to like this plan better than my idea of lighting a fire under your stuntman with the pregnancy news, but it's up to you what you want to say."

When Odele explained what she had in mind, Chiara nodded and then added her own twist…

* * *

By the next morning, Chiara was both nervous and excited. She felt as if she was jumping off a cliff—in fact, it was not so different from doing a movie stunt.

Sitting in a chair in her den facing Melody Banyon, she smoothed her hands down the legs of her slacks. It was almost a replay of her last interview with the reporter...except Rick wasn't here.

"Are you pregnant?"

There it was. She was about to give her confirmation to the world. "Yes, I am."

"Congratulations."

"I'm still in my first trimester."

"And how are you feeling?"

Chiara sucked in a shaky breath. "Good. A little queasy but that's normal."

Melody tilted her head and waited.

"Even though this pregnancy was unexpected," she went on, "I've always wanted children. And, you know, I've learned you can't plan everything in life."

"You were dating a stuntman working on one of your movies. Rick Serenghetti?"

"Yes. Rick did me an enormous favor. It started as a PR stunt. Rick was supposed to pose as my boyfriend to distract the press from stories about my father and his gambling. I know celebrities aren't supposed to admit to doing things for publicity, but I want to clear the air."

This was *so* hard. But she had to do it. Odele had convinced her to talk honestly about her feelings for

Rick, but Chiara had thought it was important to come clean publicly about the whole charade. Risky, but important.

"You say *started...*"

"Even though I didn't know it, Rick signed up for our make-believe because he also wanted to protect me from a stalker. It was a threat that I wasn't taking seriously enough."

"But Todd Jeffers is now charged with serious crimes. Are you relieved?"

"Yes, of course. And I'm so grateful to Rick for tackling Jeffers when he broke into my house."

"And how is your father doing?"

"Great. We met, and he agreed to go into rehab for his addiction. I'm proud of him." She had Rick to thank there, too.

Melody leaned forward. "So with your father addressing his addiction, and your stalker behind bars, you and Rick are...?"

Chiara gave a nervous laugh. "Somewhere along the way, I fell in love with Rick. I love him."

Melody leaned forward and shut off her voice recorder. "Perfect."

Chiara blew a breath. "You think so?"

The reporter gave her a sympathetic look. "I know so. A headline will appear on the *WE Magazine* site in a few hours, and then we'll go to press with the print edition for the end of the week."

Hours. That's all she had before Rick and the world would know what lay in her heart.

Best to keep occupied. She still needed to put in motion the last part of the plan, which she'd suggested to Odele.

Rick nearly fell out of his seat. *I love him.*

He'd followed the news link to *WE Magazine* in Odele's text and got a sucker punch.

Looking around his now nearly bare and sparsely furnished rental, he felt the swoosh of air that he normally associated with a high-altitude stunt.

His cell phone rang, and it was Melody Banyon from *WE Magazine.*

"Do you have a public comment on Chiara Feran's interview with us? She confirmed her pregnancy."

Yes. No. I don't know. "I won't ask how you got my number."

"I think you know the answer," Melody replied, amusement in her voice.

Odele, of course.

And then with sudden clarity, he realized going for broke was the thing to do. His concerns about privacy, getting manipulated by the press, or even publicity-hungry actresses, flew out the window. He didn't have time to think about whether this was another of Odele's PR moves. He was done with charades, make-believe and pretend.

"Anything you'd like to say for the record?" Melody prompted again.

"Yes. My feelings for Chiara were real from the beginning. There was no pretending on my part."

"And the baby news?"

Yeah, wow. Somehow tomorrow was today…but he couldn't be more elated with every passing day. "It may not have been planned, but I'm happy about it."

"Are you Prince Charming?"

He laughed ruefully. "I've enjoyed my privacy up until now. And I've liked keeping my aliases under wraps, but things are becoming public knowledge."

Melody cleared her throat. "Okay, off the record now… I wouldn't let Chiara get away if I were you. She's scared, but I've seen you two together. You belong together."

"And here I thought Chiara and I had done a good snow job convincing you that we really were a couple."

"Not as good a snow job as you two have done on each other," Melody replied.

Yeah. And suddenly he knew he had to follow through on the idea that Jordan had given him…

"Give me until tomorrow before you publish my comment, Melody. I want Chiara to be the first to know."

"Of course!" the reporter responded with a smile in her voice.

Rick barely heard her. His mind was already buzzing with ideas for props for his next stunt.

Chiara was tense. Controlling one's image was paramount in Hollywood, and she'd just blown her cover. *I love him…* And the entire world knew. There was nowhere to hide.

She wrung her hands as she stared out her kitchen

window. *WE Magazine* had published parts of her interview online late yesterday. It had been hours…and still no word from Rick.

He could humiliate her. He could issue a stunning rejection that handed her heart back to her.

Picking up the phone, she made a lifeline call to her manager.

"Oh, Odele, what have you gotten me into?" she moaned.

"Have you looked at social media?"

"Are you kidding? It's the last thing I can bring myself to peek at."

"Well, you should. The confirmation of your pregnancy has taken the internet by storm, of course."

"Great," she said weakly.

"Yup, but the viral storm is turning in your favor, sweetie. People are applauding your honesty."

"About being a fraud?"

"You were honest about the phoniness of celebrity culture."

Chiara closed her eyes. She'd gone viral as a recovering liar…and people loved it. "I'm afraid to leave the house."

"You weren't scared when you had a stalker, but now you are?"

Of course she was. She hadn't heard from Rick. The ax could still fall.

Then a distant sound reached her, and she frowned. "Hold on, Odele."

It sounded like hoof beats. *Impossible.*

She peeked out the window. A rider on a white horse was coming up the drive.

The *clomp* of hooves sounded louder as horse and rider came closer. It couldn't be…but her heart knew it was. "Odele… I've got to go."

"What's the matter, honey?" Chiara could practically hear the frown in her manager's voice. "Do I need to send the police?"

"Um, that won't be necessary. I think I'm being rescued…"

"What…?"

"It's Rick on a white horse…bye."

"Well, I'll be damned. And he didn't even give me a heads-up so I could send a photographer to snap the moment."

"We'll do the scene over for you."

"Great, because romances are my favorite."

"I'd never have known from the way you've pushed me to do action flicks—"

"And you met a hunky stuntman in the process."

"Odele, I have to go!"

Her manager laughed. "Good luck, honey."

Rushing to the front door, Chiara took a moment to glance at herself in the hall mirror. Her eyes were bright, but she wished she could have looked more polished than she did in stretch pants and a T-shirt. Still, at least these clothes continued to fit her.

She took a deep breath and opened the door, stepping outside.

Rick stopped his horse in front of her, a smile playing at his lips.

Chiara placed her hands on her hips. "You got a horse through my front gate…really?"

"I still have the code. You've got to change it if you don't want to keep having unexpected visitors."

She nodded at the animal that he sat astride, her insides buzzing. "And you rode him along canyon roads to my house?"

"Hey, I'm a stuntman."

She met his gaze head-on. "And this is one of your stunts?"

"Jordan told me to get on a horse. Before I could do it or go with the backup plan of coming by with a wood boyfriend for Ruby, you had your interview with *WE Magazine*," he said, not answering her directly. "But I thought I'd…accommodate you anyway."

She tilted her head. "Accommodate how?"

He swung down, all lithe physique, and then pulled her into his arms and kissed her.

She leaned into him, kissing him back.

When they broke apart, he said, "I love you."

She blinked back sudden emotion, and joked, "You should if you rode a horse here."

"It took me a while to recognize it, but then you were put in danger by Jeffers." His face blazed with emotion. "Damn it, Chiara, I could have lost you."

She nodded, swallowing against the lump in her throat.

"I let my experience with Isabel color my perspective even though it was becoming increasingly obvious you couldn't be more different."

She gave a watery smile. "Well, you can be forgiven for that one. Thanks to Odele, I was using you to manipulate the press, too."

"In the beginning, yeah. But you had guts and determination. Plus more and more layers that I wanted to uncover even though I kept trying to pigeonhole you as just another evil starlet."

"Who, me? Snow White?" she said playfully.

He cracked a smile and then gave her another quick kiss.

She braced her hands on his chest. "Thank you for tackling Jeffers…twice. I didn't take the risk seriously enough because I wasn't going to let you tell me what to do. But you helped me save my father from himself." When he started to say something, she placed a finger on his lips to stop him. "Thank you for coming into my life and dealing with all the craziness of fame. I was so afraid of being vulnerable and getting hurt."

He grasped her wrist and kissed her hand.

"I love you. I was falling in love with you and it scared me to feel so much," she finished.

"We're getting married."

She gave an emotional laugh—happiness bubbling out of her. "Before or after the baby is born?"

"Before. Vegas, even. Your father can give you away."

"He doesn't want to give me away. He just got me back! And I can't be an actress eloping to Vegas. It's too clichéd," she protested.

"You're a pregnant Hollywood actress who'll be

a few months along at the wedding. You're already a cliché." He winked. "We'll leave people guessing about whether we're taking our stunt to the extreme by actually getting married."

"So our love isn't real?"

"Snow, if my feelings were any more real, they'd be jumping around like the Seven Dwarves."

"Funny, Serenghetti."

And then he proceeded to show her just how real they were…

Epilogue

Two months later...

Chiara mingled with other Serenghettis who'd gathered for Serg's sixty-seventh birthday barbecue on a hot August afternoon in Welsdale. She was still getting used to these family get-togethers. They were a world apart from her past experiences with her own family. Serg and Camilla's home brimmed with animated voices and laughter.

Still, her relationship with her father had come a long way. Her father was in rehab, but he'd already announced he'd like to become an addiction counselor. And Odele had been and continued to be like a second mother. She'd already started shopping for baby clothes. And now, of course, Chiara had the Serenghettis, as well.

"The food is delicious," Marisa announced as she stepped onto the patio bathed in late-afternoon sun. "I feel even more like an overstuffed piñata."

Chiara smiled at her sister-in-law. "Now, there's a metaphor for being pregnant I haven't heard before."

In a nice surprise, shortly after her own pregnancy had gone public, Cole and Marisa had quietly announced they were expecting, too. Her sister-in-law was only a month further along. Naturally, Chiara thought, there'd be another female Serenghetti to take this journey with.

Marisa sighed. "I know what a chicken cordon bleu feels like."

"A ham?" Jordan asked, having overheard.

His sister-in-law shot him a droll look. "Funny."

"Just don't have a surprise birth," Jordan teased. "Mom wants a chance to plan for a big event for once."

Chiara bit back another smile, and then looked down at her plain platinum wedding band and large canary diamond solitaire engagement ring. She and Rick had had a quick wedding in Las Vegas with just immediate family present. It had been small, intimate and private, just like they'd wanted. There'd been no press, though they'd given Melody an exclusive after the fact.

Now as Marisa and Jordan stepped away, Rick came up and settled his hands on her shoulders, kneading them gently. Chiara nearly purred with contentment.

"How are you feeling?" Rick asked in a low voice.

"Like my next role should be as a pregnant stunt-woman," she responded.

"You'd be great. I've got just the vehicle."

"I feel like a starlet who has slept her way to the top with the studio boss."

He chuckled. "Snow, we're partners now."

At home and at the office. She and Rick were starting their own production company. He'd vowed to support her career in any way he could, and that included helping her find appropriate acting roles. For her part, she wanted to respect Rick's preference to not be in the glare of celebrity. She'd done interviews herself, but he'd insisted that as her prince, he needed and wanted to be her escort to public events.

Just then, Serafina, Marisa's cousin, stepped onto the patio and then frowned as she spotted Jordan.

"Uh-oh," Rick said in a low voice for Chiara's ears only. "Trouble."

As if on cue, Jordan gave a lazy grin, and then sauntered toward Serafina with a gleam in his eye.

Chiara smiled. "Only the best kind for those two." Then turning, she snuggled against Rick as he draped an arm around her shoulders. "Don't you agree?"

Her husband winked and gave her a kiss. "Definitely. You're the best trouble I ever had, Snow. And then love had walked in for us."

* * * * *

*If you loved this story, don't miss
Cole Serenghetti's story*

SECOND CHANCE WITH THE CEO

*Then pick up these other sexy and emotional reads
from* USA TODAY *bestselling author Anna DePalo!*

*HAVING THE TYCOON'S BABY
UNDER THE TYCOON'S PROTECTION
TYCOON TAKES REVENGE
CAPTIVATED BY THE TYCOON
AN IMPROPER AFFAIR
CEO'S MARRIAGE SEDUCTION
HIS BLACK SHEEP BRIDE
ONE NIGHT WITH PRINCE CHARMING
IMPROPERLY WED*

Available now from Harlequin Desire!

* * *

*If you're on Twitter, tell us what you think of
Harlequin Desire! #harlequindesire*

#2527 THE BABY FAVOR
Billionaires and Babies • by Andrea Laurence
CEO Mason Spencer and his wife are headed for divorce when an old promise changes their plans. They are now the guardians for Spencer's niece...and they must remain married. Will this be their second chance, one that leads to forever?

#2528 LONE STAR BABY SCANDAL
Texas Cattleman's Club: Blackmail • by Lauren Canan
When sexy former rodeo champion turned billionaire Clay Everett sets his sights on his spunky secretary, he's sure he holds the reins in their affair. Until he learns Sophie Prescott is carrying his child. Now all bets are off!

#2529 HIS UNEXPECTED HEIR
Little Secrets • by Maureen Child
After a fling with a sexy marine leaves Rita pregnant, her attempts to reach the billionaire are met with silence...until now! Brooding, reclusive Jack offers to marry Rita—in name only. Will his new family give him the heart to embrace life—and love—again?

#2530 PREGNANT BY THE BILLIONAIRE
The Locke Legacy • by Karen Booth
Billionaire Sawyer Locke only makes commitments to his hotel empire—until he meets fiery PR exec Kendall Ross. Now he can't get her out of his mind—or out of his bed. But when she becomes pregnant, will he claim the heir he never expected?

#2531 BEST FRIEND BRIDE
In Name Only • by Kat Cantrell
CEO Jonas Kim must stop his arranged marriage—by arranging a marriage for himself! His best friend, Vivian, will be his wife and never fall in love, or so he thinks. Can he keep his heart safe when Viv tempts him to become friends with benefits?

#2532 CLAIMING THE COWGIRL'S BABY
Red Dirt Royalty • by Silver James
Rancher Kaden inherited a birth father, a powerful last name and wealth—none of which he wants. His pregnant lover, debutante Pippa Duncan, has lost everything due to a dark family secret. Their marriage of convenience may undo the pain of their families' pasts, but will it lead to love?

Get 2 Free Books,
Plus 2 Free Gifts—
just for trying the Reader Service!

HARLEQUIN *Desire*

HDI7

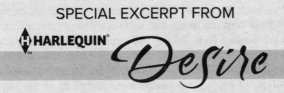
*After a fling with a sexy marine leaves Rita pregnant,
her attempts to reach the billionaire are met with
silence...until now! Brooding, reclusive Jack offers to
marry Rita—in name only. Will his new family give him
the heart to embrace life—and love—again?*

*Read on for a sneak peek of
LITTLE SECRETS: HIS UNEXPECTED HEIR
by USA TODAY bestselling author Maureen Child.*

Jack didn't make a habit of coming here. Memories were
thick and he tended to avoid them, because remembering
wouldn't get him a damn thing. But against his will, images
filled his mind.

Every damn moment of that time with Rita was etched
into his brain in living, vibrant color. He could hear the
sound of her voice. The music of her laughter. He saw the
shine in her eyes and felt the silk of her touch.

"And you've been working for months to forget it," he
reminded himself in a mutter. "No point in dredging it up
now."

What they'd found together all those months ago was
over. There was no going back. He'd made a promise to
himself. One he intended to keep.

It was a hard lesson to learn, but he had learned it in the
hot, dry sands of a distant country. And that lesson haunted
him to this day.

But Jack Buchanan didn't surrender to the dregs of fear, so he kept walking, made himself notice the everyday world pulsing around him. Along the street, a pair of musicians was playing for the crowd and the dollar bills tossed into an open guitar case. Shop owners had tables set up outside their storefronts to entice customers and, farther down the street, a line snaked from a bakery's doors all along the sidewalk.

He hadn't been downtown in months, so he'd never seen the bakery before. Apparently, though, it had quite the loyal customer base. Dozens of people—from teenagers to career men and women—waited patiently to get through the open bakery door. As he got closer, amazing scents wafted through the air and he understood the crowds gathering. Idly, Jack glanced through the wide, shining front window at the throng within, then stopped dead as an all-too-familiar laugh drifted to him.

Everything inside Jack went cold and still. He hadn't heard that laughter in months, but he'd have known it anywhere. Throaty, rich, it made him think of long hot nights, silk sheets and big brown eyes staring up into his in the darkness.

He'd tried to forget her. Had, he'd thought, buried the memories; yet now they came roaring back, swamping him until Jack had to fight for breath.

Even as he told himself it couldn't be her, Jack was bypassing the line and stalking into the bakery.

Don't miss
LITTLE SECRETS: HIS UNEXPECTED HEIR
by USA TODAY *bestselling author Maureen Child,*
available July 2017 wherever
Harlequin® Desire books and ebooks are sold.

www.Harlequin.com

HARLEQUIN® Desire

AVAILABLE JULY 2017

LONE STAR BABY SCANDAL

BY

LAUREN CANAN

PART OF THE SIZZLING
TEXAS CATTLEMAN'S CLUB: BLACKMAIL SERIES

When sexy former rodeo champion turned billionaire Clay Everett
sets his sights on his spunky secretary, he's sure he holds the reins
in their affair. Until he learns Sophie Prescott is carrying his child.
Now all bets are off!

AND DON'T MISS A SINGLE INSTALLMENT OF

TEXAS CATTLEMAN'S CLUB:

BLACKMAIL

No secret—or heart—is safe in Royal, Texas...

HARLEQUIN®

A *Romance* FOR EVERY MOOD™

Love the Harlequin book you just read?

Your opinion matters.

Review this book on your favorite
book site, review site, blog or your own
social media properties and share
your opinion with other readers!

Be sure to connect with us at:
Harlequin.com/Newsletters
Facebook.com/HarlequinBooks
Twitter.com/HarlequinBooks